WHEN DARKNESS LOVES US

ELIZABETH ENGSTROM grew up in Park Ridge, Illinois (a Chicago suburb where she lived with her father) and Kaysville, Utah (north of Salt Lake City, where she lived with her mother). After graduating from high school in Illinois, she ventured west in a serious search for acceptable weather, eventually settling in Honolulu. She attended college and worked as an advertising copywriter.

After eight years on Oahu, she moved to Maui, found a business partner, and opened an advertising agency. One husband, two children, and five years later, she sold the agency to her partner and had enough seed money to try her hand at full-time fiction writing, her lifelong dream. With the help of her mentor, science fiction great Theodore Sturgeon, *When Darkness Loves Us* was published. Since then, she has written fifteen additional books and taught the art of fiction in Oregon colleges and at writers' conferences and conventions around the world.

Engstrom moved to Oregon in 1986, where she lives with her husband Al Cratty, the legendary muskie fisherman. An introvert at heart, she still emerges into public occasionally to teach a class in novel or short story writing, or to speak at a writers' convention or conference. Learn more at www.elizabethengstrom.com

GRADY HENDRIX is a novelist and screenwriter whose books include *Horrorstör, My Best F* ....
history of the paperb'
Paperbacks from Hell,
www.gradyhendrix.

GW00566912

Cover: The cover pain
cover of the 1986 To
a paperback horror c
A Quiet Night of Fear
Baby. Since then, she has painted covers for everyone from Harlan Ellison to Ramsey Campbell, as well as dozens of magazine covers and illustrations. She's also the original scary doll painter, a trope that would soon transform paperback racks into a veritable toy store of terror. Refusing to paint the dead bodies and severed limbs her art directors demanded, Bauman used dolls instead, and as the genre got more bloodthirsty, her covers became littered with them. Her first dead doll cover was for Alan Ryan's *The Kill* (1982).

ELIZABETH ENGSTROM

With a new introduction by
GRADY HENDRIX

VALANCOURT BOOKS

Dedication: To Michael and Bill. And Evan.

When Darkness Loves Us by Elizabeth Engstrom
Originally published in hardcover by William Morrow in 1985
Reprinted as a Tor paperback in 1986
First Valancourt Books edition 2019

Published by Valancourt Books, Richmond, Virginia
http://www.valancourtbooks.com

ISBN 978-1-948405-31-7 *(trade paperback)*

Also available as an electronic book.

All Valancourt Books publications are printed on acid free
paper that meets all ANSI standards for archival quality paper.

Cover text design by M. S. Corley
Set in Dante MT

INTRODUCTION

A twelve year old girl in a one-piece swimsuit lies on her bed in a suburban bedroom. She's reading Robert Heinlein's *Have Spacesuit, Will Travel*, and *Tanar of Pellucidar* by Edgar Rice Burroughs, and *Tarzan and the Ant Men* by Edgar Rice Burroughs, and *Warlord of Mars* by Edgar Rice Burroughs, and everything by Shirley Jackson, and Edgar Allan Poe, and Octavia Butler, and Ray Bradbury, and Alfred Hitchcock's horror anthologies, and romance novels, and all of Ian Fleming's James Bond books, and anything she can get her hands on, she's shoving them all into her eyes, one after the other, all summer long.

"The only time I put on clothes," Elizabeth Engstrom says, "was to ride my bike to the library to get more books."

After that summer, "My head was bulging with fiction, and my soul and my heart were aching to spit out my own fiction, but I was too young. I didn't have anything to say."

Splitting her time between her divorced parents' homes in Chicago and Utah, the minute she turned 18, Engstrom, then named Betsy Lynn Gutzmer, ditched the mainland and moved to Honolulu, "searching for better weather." After eight years on Oahu, she moved to Maui, working for a radio station, and then for the only advertising agency on the island until she and the art director decided they could do it better on their own. The two of them teamed up and founded Baney, Gutzmer Inc. where they had their own clients and eventually did well enough to open a branch on the Big Island. Gutzmer wrote advertising copy, and pitched jobs, and she drank.

"I hung with the underbelly of society," she says. "And the worse they were, the better I felt about myself. I had friends in really low places, and they were the people I was comfortable with. No real identity, living in the shadows, only coming out at night."

For ten years, Gutzmer was a drunk. And then in 1980, she stopped. Full of pent-up, raw emotions that had no outlet, she found a writers' group consisting of four other women. They based their process on Peter Elbow's "teacherless writing class" in which everyone reads each other's work and then tries to give the writer some sense of how their story was experienced by each reader. For five years, these five women met every single week, during which time Gutzmer published a few short stories here and there—in Crispin Burnham's *Eldritch Tales* zine, in one of Maui's community college's literary journals. But until she went to Disneyland, nothing clicked.

By now, Gutzmer was sober, married and had adopted her husband's two children, and when the family went on vacation to Disneyland she rode the *20,000 Leagues Under the Sea* attraction and had a full-blown panic attack.

"You can see from the top that nobody's even submerged," she says. "It just goes around a track in the pool. But I was inside and suddenly there wasn't enough air for me and everyone else, and I wanted to claw my way out."

The idea hit her almost fully formed: what if she was trapped underground and pregnant? The novella poured out of her and she submitted "When Darkness Loves Us" to Theodore Sturgeon's writing workshop. You can read his reaction in the other foreword to this edition, but he did more than admit her to the workshop, he found her an agent. Sandra Dijkstra signed Betsy Lynn Gutzmer, now writing under the name Elizabeth Engstrom (her married name combined with her daughter's middle name, Elizabeth), and Dijkstra told her that if they had another novella they could submit the two together as a book.

Engstrom had already written "Beauty Is . . ." which was based on a real-life incident. On Maui, a developmentally disabled woman had gotten a job at Kentucky Fried Chicken, a relatively progressive employer at the time. A group of guys started harassing her on her daily walk to work and she didn't know how to make them stop. They started inviting her to a bar. And getting her drunk. And taking advantage of her.

"I was horrified," Engstrom remembers. "I thought, did I want to live in a world where things like that happened?"

Together, the two novellas were sold at auction to William Morrow. They wanted a third story to round out the volume, but Engstrom didn't have anything she liked enough. Didn't matter. There were hardcover sales, book club sales, European rights sales, and a sale to Tor for the paperback edition (with a now-classic cover by artist Jill Bauman). "Beauty Is . . ." would go on to be optioned twice for film.

But on Hawaii, Engstrom felt like an outcast. Racially she was *haole*, a non-Hawaiian, and on top of that she was from the Mainland, and to her the chasm that separated her from other Hawaiians seemed unbridgeable. So in 1986, she moved to Eugene, Oregon and two years later she delivered *Black Ambrosia*, her first novel, and her agent dropped her.

Told from the point of view of Angelina, a teenaged girl who decides she's a vampire, *Black Ambrosia* is set in a rundown America where everyone's clinging to the last rung on the economic ladder. Angelina walks the cold shoulders of filthy highways looking for warm blood in fleabag motels and soulless suburbs. She's a classical vampire who hates crucifixes, turns into fog, sleeps in a coffin, and controls men's minds. But she might also just be a teenaged girl who's losing her mind.

"Sometimes teenaged girls can talk themselves into doing things and being things by the sheer force of their personalities," Engstrom says. "What if a girl talked herself into becoming a vampire? She discovers she has power over men and she wants to become this thing, and so she does."

After all, Angelina discovers (or, rather, decides) she's a vampire after a harrowing attempted rape, and every chapter is anchored by a closing, italicized portion of the text told from a different character's point of view, retelling the events of the previous chapter with all reference to the supernatural removed, offering up a mundane counter-narrative where Angelina is just a psychopathic serial killer.

Dijkstra told Engstrom that if this was her idea of fiction, she wasn't the agent for her. But Tor editor Melissa Ann Singer had loved *When Darkness Loves Us* and she bought *Black Ambrosia* (and commissioned a cover by Bob Eggleton). Tor would remain Engstrom's publisher for her 1991 *Lizzie Borden* novel and her 1992 collection of tiny, almost fable-sized short stories, *Nightmare Flower*.

Engstrom is still writing, but with *When Darkness Loves Us* and *Black Ambrosia* she delivered three of the best monster stories ever written. Weirdly enough, they were written around the same time that Clive Barker was busy writing his *Books of Blood* which are largely based on the notion that monsters didn't have to be scary, but could also be figures of pity, romance, or awe. Monsters had their own point-of-view, one which Engstrom embraced hard, making her creatures simultaneously predatory and pathetic.

Barely out of their teens, Sally Ann Hixson in "When Darkness Loves Us" and Angelina in *Black Ambrosia* exist in the margins, one of them trapped in a series of underground tunnels, the other trapped outside humanity by her blood lust. Circumstances push them far beyond their capabilities, and their humanity, and they find themselves doing things they never could have imagined to survive. But these harrowing ordeals don't break them, they imbue them with a monstrous strength. Finding their power in the margins, being outsiders suits them.

"Somebody told me writers only have one story to tell," Engstrom says. "And that's our story. And we dress it up in different clothes and different times and places, but it's still our story."

When she moved to Hawaii, Engstrom had become an outsider, and also a monster.

"You think you're cool when you can drink more than anyone else," she says. "And you start to become the monster a little bit. You start to do terrible things to people and you justify that in your mind saying, 'I was drunk at the time.' You become the monster, then you justify the monster, then you glorify the monster."

Both *Black Ambrosia* and "When Darkness Loves Us" reflect the monster as a creature of both incredible strength and grotesque weakness, but "Beauty Is . . ." goes further. Its main character, Martha, is developmentally disabled and was born without a nose. Her stunted mental capacity and her facial deformity brand her as a monster, but then some local gutterpunks start getting her drunk and it feels like the story is about to crow, "Who's the real monster now?"

But Engstrom isn't interested in a simple switcheroo. Instead, Martha is saved from humiliation and finds friends, and a lover, and the more she's loved, the more her mind begins to heal itself, until she's reading, and handling her own finances. As she's welcomed into the community, she sheds her monstrosity and becomes just another citizen. When she's treated with love and compassion, Martha is a person, when she's treated with hatred and contempt, she's a monster. And, like all monsters, she's a mirror.

Engstrom's first three stories are full of monsters, not just Angelina, but the man who hunts her until murdering Angelina becomes a cancer that consumes his life. Not just Sally Ann Hixson but her husband who patronizes her, and her son who takes advantage of her inability to say "no" to him. Not just Martha, but her father who rejects her cruelly, and the people who exploit her. If a monster is merely something that goes further than we dared dream possible—stronger, crueler, uglier, more obsessed—then Engstrom's stories crawl with them. Because in this world there is always a monster. And often, the monster is you.

GRADY HENDRIX
February 2019

FOREWORD

I wish you could have been there. Yes, I mean you. Let me tell you where, and why.

My wife, whom you'll call Lady Jayne as soon as you see her—as I did—my wife and I had come to an island in the middle of the Pacific Ocean to teach writing. We entered a huge room in a house that overlooks macadamia and cane fields, and is surrounded by papaya and banana trees and a symphonic riot of flowers; and there we met our class.

And Betsy.

Pretty exotic. Oh sure—Maui with its puffs of rain cloud and the dark flanks of its sleeping volcanoes wearing their rumpled capes of pool-table felt, its long-tailed firebirds and impudent mynas, its kaleidoscopic ethnics and accents, and its unfailing—what—*smilingness*: It's exotic all right.

Except Betsy.

Elizabeth Engstrom is not exotic. She is a married woman with a nice husband and two great kids and a tidy home and a quiet voice with which she would no more shout than she would ride a motorcycle into one's living room. She spoke seldom during the course we taught; when she did, it was to the point and rather noticeably her own opinion and none other, prevailing or not. Her greatest eloquence, which we both noticed from that first entrance, was a pair of eyes two clicks brighter than the brightest you have ever seen. These transmitted something quite beyond words—an intensity to learn and to understand and to *do*. This woman meant to get into print. Revise that. I shouldn't have said "intensity"; I should have said "ferocity."

This class was extraordinary. None had seen print: At this writing six of them are writing and selling, and much as we'd like to take credit, we must assert that all we had to do was scratch lightly and the talent exploded all over the place.

We workshopped manuscripts. (*Workshop* has become a verb.) Betsy's twenty-odd-thousand-word story had to be put off while we went through the maze of story architecture, mood, crisis/climax/denouement, the "sound" of punctuation and all that machine-shop stuff, until the last meeting, when we had Betsy read her story aloud.

It was *When Darkness Loves Us*.

It was for this moment that I wish you had been there.... There is a thing that happens in theater when one or another of the cast is having "his" or "her" night—a very special spell that overtakes a performer; you can tell when it's happening by two things. One, you become aware that everyone else in the cast is playing to and for the magicked one. And two, when the final curtain falls, instead of the appreciative crash of applause, there is an instant of hush before anyone moves. It's the possibility of that hush that keeps actors—actors.

Well, that's what happened at that reading.

Later, on the mainland, we got a look at *Beauty Is* ... Our immediate reaction was to get it launched. The two stories together made a generous-enough bookful *but* they were not connected in any way. Betsy said I was crazy but I said, "Do it." Her able agent said I was crazy but I said, "Do it." Her publisher probably thought the same ... but the publisher did it.

And now I envy you, and anyone else who has not, but who is about to, meet Elizabeth Engstrom. Behind that soft-voiced style is power, is surprise, is—well, that ferocity I mentioned. You are now introduced.

THEODORE STURGEON

Oregon, 1984

ACKNOWLEDGMENTS

A writer needs sustenance in many ways during differing phases of a work. Of these, I believe, dialogue is the most nourishing. I have been fortunate.

Lifeblood was contributed by Clarice Cox, Ted and Jayne Sturgeon, Maggie Doran, Madge Walls, Marie Johnson, Tonia Baney, and Shelley Nalepa, to name only a few.

Thanks to John Briley for accuracy, Sandra Dijkstra for direction, and to Ted Sturgeon for the right hug at the right time.

And a note of specific gratitude to my folks, for teaching me that molds are for plastic.

WHEN DARKNESS
LOVES US

PART ONE

I

Sally Ann Hixson, full with the blush of spring and gleeful playfulness as only sixteen-year-olds know it, hid around the side of the huge tree at the edge of the woods as the great tractor drove past her. She saw her husband, torso bare, riding the roaring monster, his smooth muscles gliding under sweat-slick skin tanned a deep brown. She didn't want him to see her . . . not yet.

She plopped down into the long grass, feeling the rough bark of the big tree against her back as she gazed into the woods. This had been her favorite place to play when she was little. She could just barely see her parents' house on the hill about a mile off. Her mother had noticed her restlessness as soon as the major canning was done and sent her away to run, to play, to spy on her new husband as he worked with her father in the fields.

This summer, they would build their house on the other hill, and they could raise their family to be good country folk, just like their fathers and their fathers before them. She stretched her legs into a sunbeam, feeling them warm under her new jeans. She had a wild impulse to cast off her clothes and run naked through the grass. She thought of Michael then, and their delicious lovemaking the night before. She was not able to give of herself very freely while in her parents' house, but some nights Michael took her by the hand and led her out to the hill where their house would soon be built, high up on the knoll, and with the moon watching and the cicadas playing the romantic background music, they would make love, uninhibited, wonderful love. They explored each other's bodies and released sensations unfamiliar to either of them, with joy and togetherness in discovering the full potentials of their sexuality.

The idea made her tingle, then blush, and she crossed her legs, thinking of the times her thoughts strayed to such matters when she was with her mother. It was worse then, because she was sure lovemaking was not like that for her parents, and sometimes she had to excuse herself and go into the bathroom until she could stop grinning.

She picked up a long strand of grass and put it between her teeth as she peeked around the tree and watched her man, handsome and tousled, drive the machine over the next hill. She glanced around one more time to make sure her pest of a little sister wasn't lurking somewhere in the shadows. She jumped up and followed the edge of the woods until she could see the flatbed truck where her father waited. Michael would stop there and have a glass of iced water that she had put in a thermos jug for him that morning. She saw him turn to look behind him, so she dodged back into the woods . . . and saw the stone steps that led down into the ground.

It was so familiar. She used to play here when she was small, but she hadn't come here in years. There were two brand-new doors with shiny hinges mounted to the concrete, and she knew that it was going to be sealed against children and mishaps forever. What used to be the attraction here so long ago? She remembered the darkness and a tunnel, and she stepped down to the first step, then the second one, looking into a black hole that had no end.

It was cool, but not cold, and she took the sweatshirt that was tied around her waist and slipped it over her shoulders. She continued down into the eerie darkness and tried to remember the story about this place. A hiding place for runaway slaves, maybe. She continued her descent. The steps were sturdy, stone set in concrete. She felt her way along with her hand, the rough rock cool to the touch. The steps were narrow, set at an easy angle, and as she glanced back to reassure herself of the warm spring day above, she noticed that the entrance to the stairs would be out of sight before she reached the bottom. Yet down she went.

At the bottom there was a hole in the side of the wall, and memories, just out of reach, began to form themselves in her mind. She wondered if any of the old playthings were still in the tunnel. She crouched down to enter. Once inside, she straightened up—the tunnel was quite large. The small amount of light afforded by the entry provided very little visibility, but she made her way slowly along the tunnel, until the toe of her tennis shoe struck something that went ringing into the darkness. It was a baby spoon. The light glinted off the surface, just enough for her to find it. She picked it up, suddenly remembering the nursery rhymes and the frightening pleasure of having tea parties in such a forbidden place.

She rubbed the spoon between her fingers: tiny, smooth, and round, with a handle that doubled back upon itself, big enough for her finger. Then she remembered Jackie, killed in Vietnam. They were inseparable, always knew they'd eventually marry, and she had cried when he went off to the army. But now Jackie was gone and Michael was up there, and she had better go surprise him before she missed her chance. With one more thought of Jackie and a prayer for his soul, she moved back through the tunnel to the hole in the wall and the stairs, back to the sun and the springtime.

She heard Michael's voice above the roar of the idling tractor just as she came through the hole in the wall, caught the last words of his sentence. Angry that he had found her before she could surprise him, she had started running up the stairs when the doors above slammed shut, cutting off all light, and the sound of a padlock's shank driving home pierced her heart. She stood stock-still. The walls instantly closed in around her, and the air disappeared. She managed one scream, drowned by the earth-vibrating essence of great engine above. She gasped, stumbled up one more step, then fell to her knees, fighting for breath, trying desperately to repress the horror of being locked in the darkness, while Michael's last words reverberated in her mind: ". . . before one of my kids falls down there."

Chest heaving, she tried to crawl up the stairs, fingers clawing—capable only of breathless moans rather than the strong screams she was trying desperately to utter in a vain attempt to bring father and husband to her rescue. She convulsed in fear, fingers stiffening, back arching. A muscular spasm turned her onto her back, the stone steps dug into her spine, and the darkness moved in and took over her mind.

The awakening was slow, starting with the pain in her lower back, then in her fingers, followed by the throbbing in her head. Slowly she opened her eyes. Darkness. She felt her eyes with her fingers to see if they were open or if she was dreaming. She felt the cold stone steps beneath her. Then she remembered. She looked around, but could see absolutely nothing. On her hands and knees, she mounted the steps until her head touched the heavy wooden doors, and she remembered the shiny new hinges and the solid, heavy wood that wouldn't rot as the seasons changed.

It must be night, she thought, or surely I could see a crack of daylight somewhere. She felt alone, isolated, abandoned. Tears leaked out the corners of her eyes as she focused all her panic and shot it to her husband, hoping that somewhere there was a God who would transmit the message to him, so he could sense her surroundings and come rescue her and take her home to their warm, soft bed.

She pushed on the door with her shoulders, and it didn't give at all. She lost hope of wiggling the hinges loose. Cold and afraid, she huddled on the first steps, knowing that soon Michael and her dad would be coming for her. It was the only possible place she could be. After she had been missing for a night, they would come looking for her here. And here she would be, brave (not really) and okay (barely) and so very glad to see them. She fought the claustrophobic feeling and tried to relax. She was desperately tired and uncomfortable. She put her head on her arms and slept.

When she awoke, it was still pitch-dark and she had to go to the bathroom. She couldn't be embarrassed by the foul smells of her own excretions when her husband came to rescue her, so she had to find some place to go. Slowly, with aching muscles, she moved crablike down the stairs, visualizing in her mind's eye the hole in the wall and the tunnel thereafter. She crouched, feeling the circumference of the hole so she wouldn't hit her head, and slipped through to the big tunnel.

She remembered that it ran wide and true to where she had picked up the spoon, and she took brave steps in the darkness. She remembered Jackie, talking to her when they were out walking in the countryside on dark moonless nights. "You'll never stumble if you walk boldly and pick your feet up high." It worked then, and it worked now. She walked through the darkness and the fear, until she sensed by the echoes around her that the tunnel took a turn to the right. In the corner she relieved herself.

Nothing could be worse than waiting at the top of the steps, so she decided to explore the tunnel just a little farther and exercise the kinks out of her legs. The tunnel wound around until she was certain she must be directly under the stairs; then it straightened again. Her breathing echoed off the walls in eerie rasps. She walked still farther, and the air turned cooler. It smelled different. Water. Suddenly overcome with thirst, she walked boldly and entered a large cavern. The change in acoustics was immediate. She felt small and lost after the intimacy of the tunnel. Pebbles crunched underfoot.

She picked up a handful of loose stones and began tossing them around her to get a bearing on the dimensions of the cavern. It was huge. A path seemed to continue right through it, water on both sides. Slowly she stepped off the right side of the path, taking baby steps down into the darkness until her tennis shoe splashed in water. She lifted a cupped handful to her nose, then tasted it. Delicious. Eagerly, with both feet in the water, she drank her fill.

Wouldn't Dad be surprised, she thought, to know of this underwater lake on his property. The water tasted like the cave smelled—mossy—but it seemed pure, and it did the trick. She splashed some on her face, stood up, and dried her hands on her sweatshirt.

Feeling far more comfortable, she picked up another handful of pebbles and started throwing them. On this side of the path was a small pond, but the lake on the other side seemed endless. She threw a rock as far as she could, and still it plopped into the water. She threw another to the side, and it splashed. She threw another and there was no sound. Her heart froze. Maybe it had landed on a moss island. She threw one more in roughly the same direction and heard it land with a plop, and she visualized the concentric circles of black ripples edging out toward her.

She walked along the path, humming away the discomfort, spraying pebbles in wide sweeping arcs. The sound was friendly. Pebbles gone, she continued walking until she could feel the cavern narrowing back into a tunnel, and it was then that she heard the splash behind her. A small splash, as if one of the pebbles had been held up from its fate, suspended, until it finally fell. She stopped, midstep, and listened. The darkness pressed in upon her, and she could hear her blood rush through her veins. Silence. She had resumed her walk, stepping quietly, when another splash came, closer behind her, and her mind again was seized with unparalleled terror. She froze. A third noise, a sucking sound coming from the water just inches away from her feet, made her start. Moans of panic churning up unbidden, she ran blindly, until she stumbled and collided at a turn with the wall of the tunnel. She wildly felt her way around the turn and continued running the length of it until the cave with its lake and resident monster were far behind her.

She stopped for breath, the tunnel becoming a close friend. She was sure of the walls around her, and there were only two directions to be concerned with. Still her heart pounded. She leaned against the wall of the tunnel in despair. The darkness was terrifying. She could dimly see some kind of tracers in front of her eyes as she passed her hand in front of her face, but could not make out even the shapes of her fingers. Her eyes ached from trying. The tears were a long time coming, beginning first with shuddering whimpers, then great, racking, soul-filled sobs. The hopelessness of the situation was overwhelming. There was no point in going on, and she could not go back past the creature in the lake. Just the thought of going back made her want to vomit. She would stay right there until she starved to death. Exhausted by the scare, the run, and the cry, eventually she slept.

She dreamed of Michael. They were running together through the waist-high grass, laughing. He tripped her, and holding her so she would not fall too hard, he came down on top of her, his face so close, and he moved as if to kiss her. Instead, he said, *"You're going to rot down there, aren't you?"*

She awoke with a piercing scream that echoed back to her again and again and again, so that even after she had stopped, she had to put her hands to her ears to keep out the terrible noise. She sat straight up, looking ahead at the darkness. "Oh, God." Her soul wrenched inside of her. "NO!" she shouted. "I WON'T rot down here! I WILL SURVIVE!" The loud sound of her voice set her heart pounding again, and she started to think clearly. The decision to survive created bravery in her, and she wanted to make a plan. She knew now that she would survive until she was rescued.

Shelter. That was a laugh. No problem. Because it was a bit warm, she rolled up her jeans to just below the knee. She certainly wasn't going to freeze. She stood and tied the sweatshirt again around her waist. Food. Now that was a problem. And she was definitely hungry. Water. If there was one lake, there must be another. Or a stream. She would continue down these tunnels until she found what she needed and then found a way out of here. She couldn't wait to be discovered. Where there was water, there was most likely food. Fish! Probably the monster in the lake was nothing more than a couple of fish, their long-undisturbed life in the lake interrupted by the stones. Maybe she could catch a fish to eat.

She thought back to her science books, to pale, sickly fish with bulging blind eyes and horrendous teeth that lived so deep in the ocean that no light penetrated their lair, and she shuddered. So much for the fish. She'd have to eat them raw anyway. No good. Moss, maybe. Seaweed was supposed to be good for you; maybe moss was just as good. Maybe also, there was a way out of here. She got up and started down the tunnel, thinking as she went, trying to ignore the gnawing in her belly that would soon, very soon, have to be satisfied.

She walked on, wondering how long she'd been there, wondering how long it would be until she heard Michael's booming voice. She would keep track of time with marks on the cave wall, but that was pretty silly, because she wouldn't be able to see them. By the number of times she slept? No good. By her menstrual periods? Nonsense. She would never be here a whole month, and besides that, she hadn't had a period in the two months she and Michael had been married.

No matter how bravely she told herself that things were going to be all right, now she had two doubts nagging the back of her mind.

She walked until her legs were leaden; then she sat and slept and walked some more. There must be miles and miles of tunnel in here. She crossed two streams, both of which had water seeping from one wall, crossing the floor of the tunnel, and leaking out the other side. Barely enough to drink—she would put her lips to the wall and suck up what moisture was needed to keep the dangerous thirst away. She knew, too, that if she didn't find something to eat soon, she would no longer have the energy to look. Her jeans were a little baggy on her already slim frame, and her steps were slower and not always in a straight line.

Sleeping when tired, she made her way through the endless tunnel with its twistings and turnings, her hands raw from catching herself after stumbling over the uneven flooring as her steps began to drag. After countless naps, with weak legs, bleeding and blistered, she tripped over a rise in the tunnel floor and lay there, her will almost gone, overcome by thirst and hunger, so tired, wanting that final sleep that would bring peace.

In half consciousness, her brain fevered and delirious, she cried out "Michael!" and her voice reverberated off the walls of a large cavern. Then she heard water dripping.

She crawled painfully toward the sound and found a pool of water, cold and delicious. She lay on her stomach and drank from her hands until she was full. It was in the half sleep that followed that Jackie came to her and brought her food. She heard his voice, and looked up. He stood over her, his face illuminated in the darkness by a glow, a radiance. "Eat these, Sally Ann. They're good for you." She picked one up. It was a fat slug, slippery on one side and rough on the other side, about the size of her thumb.

"I can't eat this."

"You can. It's good for you. You have to. Pop the whole thing in your mouth like a cherry tomato and bite once, then swallow. It's easy. Here. Try." Too tired to feel revulsion, she put the slug into her mouth and chomped down hard. She felt it burst, squirting down her throat and she swallowed quickly, followed by a handful of cold water. Yuck. It tasted awful. He encouraged her to eat more, and she did. She finished all those he had brought her and, stomach full, slept where she lay.

3

"Jackie?"

"Hmmm?"

"Are you a ghost?"

"I don't know."

The question had burned in her mind since she had first seen him the day he'd saved her. Fearing the worst— that she was mad—she had promised herself not to ask the question until he had been with her for a while.

"Well, how did you come to be here? And why can I see you when I can't even see my hands in front of my face?"

"I don't know that either, Sally Ann. All I know is that I was in Vietnam, and we were carrying wounded back to the camp. There was a yell and some sniper fire. I got hit in the chest . . . and the next thing I knew was that you were dying and I had to find some food for you to eat. I can see you, too, you know. It is pretty strange."

"The Vietnam war ended more than five years ago, Jackie. You were killed there."

This bit of news seemed no surprise to him. They sat in the main cavern with their backs up against the wall, comfortable on a mattress of soft dry moss that Sally had gathered for their bed. Her pregnancy was confirmed—there was no other explanation for the growing bulge in her belly—and she had stopped wearing her jeans long ago.

It had taken her a long time to recover, but Jackie helped nurse her back to health. His devotion to her, and the baby she carried, helped her accept the fact that unless Michael found his way to her, she was stuck for the time being. The resiliency of youth healed her body and her mind. She adapted to her new surroundings as best she could, and as time went on, she pined less and less for her family.

Jackie urged her on, and together they explored the immediate regions of their homestead, discovered many large tunnels and smaller tributaries. One led to a swift-running stream, and it was here that Sally made her toilet. Another entered a monstrous cavern like a hollowed-out mountain, with sheer drops of hundreds or more feet, as she estimated by dropping rocks from their ledges.

A smaller cavern revealed what seemed to be thousands of skeletons. The final resting place, Sally Ann speculated, of all those slaves trying to escape. How long did they search for a way out before they sat down together and starved to death? What a terrible way to die. Lost, sightless, terrified. Their remains were a fortunate discovery, however, for from these bones Jackie and Sally fashioned plenty of useful tools—bowls, knives, awls, and supports. It also reaffirmed her will to survive.

This same cavern yielded mushrooms of many flavors. Sally found the mushroom patch by stepping on the spongy fungi as she walked carefully around, searching the area. Just as she found the mushrooms, Jackie discovered a tough razorlike lichen growing around the walls. Sally had begun the dangerous habit of tasting everything that smelled okay. She couldn't help herself. Sometimes the cravings were just too intense. The mushrooms didn't hurt her, and when she soaked the lichen, it too became palatable.

It was strange how she could see Jackie as he worked; he seemed so old, so smart. The only time her eyes hurt her now was when she was exploring a new region, straining vainly to see where she was stepping. Sometimes she just closed them and wandered. It made no difference. She could see Jackie and nothing else, eyes open or closed.

She still became frightened, especially when Jackie went away. He went off on exploration trips of his own at times, mostly when he sensed she needed to be alone. The fear was not of the caverns, though, nor of monsters (even though the lake creature continued to haunt her dreams) or bogeymen. The fear seeped in when she was reflecting on her past life—Michael, her mother, father, and sister. The fear told her that she would be here until she died, that her child and its father would never meet. When the fear came, and she started to pant with the physical effect, and her eyes bulged in the darkness, looking from side to side trying to find a way out, Jackie would come back and sit with her, and soon the calm would descend. They became very close.

There was always plenty of food. Sally had merely to pick the slugs from the walls, wash them in the pond, and eat. There was also a kind of kelp that grew on the edges of the rocks in the water and on the sides of the tunnel where the water ran down, and now and then a fish would float up, and she would ravenously eat it, bones and all.

The water level fluctuated, dramatically at times. Sometimes when they went to sleep the water would be low, but when they awoke, it would reach almost to their bed. Now and then they would find things floating in it: Apples sometimes showed up, even a cabbage once; frequently there were walnuts and an occasional dead rodent, all of which added up to an adequate diet.

Their bed was comfortable; they were dry, clean, warm, fed, and together. And it was at times like this that they philosophized about their predicament—she being both grateful and angry.

Sally Ann was a fairly responsible sort of a girl, level-headed and born with an instinct to roll with the punches. That's how she felt about their situation. They had to make the best of it. What concerned her most, though, was the birth of her child. What to name him? How to keep from losing him in the dark? Jackie seemed convinced it was to be a son, and Sally Ann had taken a liking to the name Clinton. It was a solid name, and had enough hard sounds to make it easily understood when she had to call to him in the darkness.

Jackie's undying cheerfulness helped chase away what blues came and went: He was totally unwilling to look at the negative side of things or talk of despair. They lay close together at sleep time and chased away the bad dreams. He even cut her hair. A tortuous process. Her blond hair was thin, and she had always worn it quite long, but in the time they spent in the underworld it had grown much too long to be manageable. It was always getting in her way and washing it was quite out of the question. She lay with her neck on her jeans, her head on a boulder; with a sharp rock, Jackie sawed away at her hair, wearing it through more than cutting it. The end result felt uneven and strange, but more comfortable.

The baby grew rapidly, and in the last days, it was too dangerous to be awkwardly stumbling around in the darkness. She confined herself to her moss mattress and contemplated Michael.

Again and again she would lapse into despair until Jackie came to lift her spirits. He told her how he had delivered babies for women in Nam, said he was experienced, that there was nothing to it, and though she didn't believe him, he talked to her in his calm, low voice until she was convinced there was nothing to fear.

But when the time came, when the pains racked her whole body, and her water broke, and she began to cry and scream and writhe on her bed, she wished for Dr. Stirling and his warm, confident hands. But Jackie was there, and he talked to her—rubbed her back between contractions and spoke of the coming baby and what a joy it would be. She thought of how happy it would make Michael to know that he had a baby, and she gritted her teeth and bore the pain and finally bore the baby. It emerged screaming and choking, and the reverberations in the cavern were joyous to hear.

She lifted the baby, warm and slippery, to her belly, and her hands moved over it to reassure herself that it was real, that it was whole and had all its parts. She discovered that it was indeed a son. Jackie brought her water in a skull bowl, and with the baby at her breast, they tied the umbilical cord with her shoelaces and severed it with a sharpened bone. He helped her deliver the afterbirth, which he put away to eat later, then cleaned up around them. He brought the fresh moss that had been stockpiled for the occasion, then lay down beside mother and son, and enshrouded in darkness, they all slept.

4

"I'm cold, Mommy."

"Well then, silly, come out of the water and I'll dry you off."

Tall as his mother's shoulder, Clint came dripping out of the pond and stood shivering by her side. She rubbed him briskly with a handful of soft dry moss to help restore circulation, then pulled him down to her lap. They sat together, rocking back and forth, naked, she appreciating the coolness of his body as he appreciated the warmth of hers. They were very close, too close at times, she thought, but she constantly had to reevaluate her standards. In such an abnormal situation, she had to trust her judgment. His mouth automatically groped for her breast, and he gently sucked on it as they sat together. Her milk had dried up long ago, but this closeness was very important.

His little body was hard, muscular, compact, with just a little potbelly protruding, and though he was small, he was strong. She often wondered about his physical development without the sun. He seemed healthy, and he certainly was happy. A joy to her, even though she had never seen his face.

"Tell me again about sun and sky." When he was a baby, Sally Ann had told him stories about his father and the place where she had lived above ground, and he never tired of hearing about the sun and the sky, the plants, meadows, fruits, and delicious things of nature.

"Morning time is when the sun comes up in the sky and makes everything bright and you can see for miles. There are woods by where my parents live, and acres and acres of wheat fields. Your daddy works in those fields and his skin is tanned and brown. He eats sweet jam that I made for him before I came here to have you."

"What's 'see' again?"

"It's another sense, honey. Like feeling or tasting or smelling. Listen. Hear that water drip? Well, if you go put your hand under it you can feel the drop, and if you could see it, it would look like a tiny jewel, a little precious piece of sunlight captured in the water. Someday you will see it. Someday your daddy will come down here and find us and take us back up to the farm and you'll be able to run in the sunlight."

"I wish he'd come soon, Mommy."

"Me too, honey." Her heart went out to this perfect child who didn't understand what seeing was, who didn't know the wonders of life and nature.

Sally Ann gathered up their things and started back to the main cavern which had been their home since Clint was born. Born to the darkness, he was naturally oriented, and ran ahead of her, totally unafraid, at peace with the elements of his underworld life. She walked along slowly. She knew that she was planting a few seeds of dissatisfaction when she talked to him of the aboveground world, that he longed to see the magic things that she talked of, but how else was she to explain

31

life to him? And she did believe that one day they would be discovered and taken back.

He was a very independent boy, and he had thoughts of his own about the world above. Sally Ann could tell he doubted that everything she talked about existed. She could hardly blame him. How could he believe in the sun when he had never even used his eyes? When she stopped to think about it, as she did now, it saddened her. She wanted all the experiences of life to be his: to run and play in the meadow, to hear the birds, to see the stars. I guess it's a little like believing in God, she thought. One has to believe, and then belief becomes strengthened. If one disbelieves, then disbelief is strengthened. And turning your back, once you know the truth, leads to evil.

She showed him her tennis shoes in an attempt to pique his curiosity, but he wasn't interested. And there wasn't anything she could do but accept it, was there?

When Clint was far enough ahead of her, she called to Jackie and he joined her on her walk. Clint couldn't see or hear Jackie, so he reserved his visiting time for Sally alone, after Clint was asleep. Many times they discussed for hours the best way to help Clint understand. Sally was confident that he was growing up to be a normal boy. He delighted in finding new kinds of life in the caves, some of which they gratefully added to their diet—like the crayfish that blindly lived in the fast-running streams—and some of which provided hours of entertainment for Clint—like the dim-witted puff-fish that would let him pick them up and transport them from one pond to another and back again. He played war games with them, playfully pitting one against the other, with food as the supreme reward. They seemed, in their cold, reptilian way, to be almost affectionate to him. But then, he was always kind to them.

Clint was crossing the swift stream on the stepping-stones when he first discovered the crayfish. He was chewing one of a handful of slugs, when one slipped out between his fingers just at the edge of the stream and he heard it splash into the water. The water began boiling with activity, and unafraid as he was, he reached in and pulled out a crayfish as long as his arm.

Jackie said that as long as it ate what you ate, it should be okay for you to eat it. So they shelled it and discovered that it was delicious. Sally Ann couldn't quite get over her fear of putting her hand right into the black water, though Clint teased her about it, but she was grateful that he would bring her those delectable treats now and then.

Yes, he was a joy to her, but in her times alone she wondered many things. What would happen to him if she died? Was she glorifying the outside world to him so that he would never rest until he saw it? Was there a way out of here? She and Jackie had searched the tunnels and caverns for years, looking for a way out, and nothing had come of it yet. She knew that the stairs were securely locked and guarded by a beast in the lake, so they avoided that direction. Maybe, though, Clint would have the hunger, the burning desire to go to the magic place she had described for him, and through some mercy from heaven, he would be shown the way out. God knows a boy shouldn't live his life in tunnels and caves.

"Why so silent?" Jackie had been walking alongside her, respecting her contemplative mood.

"What is the purpose of all this, Jackie? Are we doing something here for someone's benefit? What possible part in God's plan are we fulfilling? I want my son out of here. We've been here for years, Jackie. YEARS! Clint is probably eight years old now, and he's never even

SEEN, for God's sake. And Michael. What must he have thought, that his young wife had run away? And my parents. And my sister. Jackie. I've got to get out of here with my child, NOW!"

Jackie looked at her sadly. "I've a feeling, Sally Ann, that all this IS for a higher purpose."

"I can't accept that. Clint and I are going to find our way out of here—NOW!" Suddenly she was filled with a sense of purpose, of immediacy. The drive had taken hold of her with a single-mindedness that demanded attention. She knew, deep in her soul, that Clint was old enough now to be a help, not a hindrance, and if they were ever going to do it, now was the time.

She ran back to the main cavern and found Clint. She grabbed his shoulders with both hands and put her face up next to his.

"Clint. We've got to get out of here. We've got to get up to the sunshine and the grass and the fresh air, and see your daddy. We can stay here forever, and we probably will, if we don't make the commitment—right NOW—to get out of here. Now I'm going to pack up some moss and some water and some food, and we're going to keep going until we find a way out of these caves. Okay? Are you ready?"

"We've never looked the other way." Sally knew he meant the way of the monster in the lake. She had never returned that way, had never gone back, had never tried the stairs again. She had chosen to stay in the caves rather than risk what might be in that lake. But now she wasn't so sure.

"Then that's the way we'll start. Get ready."

They didn't speak again until they each had bundles tied to their backs and had entered the tunnel forbidden to Clint all his life. Then he said, "Why now, all of a

34

sudden? You were happy here until now. Don't you want to be down here with me anymore?"

"Of course I want to be with you, honey. There are just better things for you than an old cave. I want to see your face. I want to see how much you look like your daddy."

"You always told me Daddy would rescue us. He hasn't, though, has he? And now you want to go find him. Why? We live here. This is our home. We're happy here. Don't you want to be with me anymore?"

Sally stopped and reached out for him, but he avoided her touch. She was astonished at his bitterness.

"Clint . . ."

"Don't! You don't want me anymore. You just want to go chasing a dream. There is no 'up there.' There is no 'daddy.' There's nothing but you and me and that's not good enough for you. You're a liar and I don't want YOU any more, either!" He ran off into the darkness.

"Clint!" She screamed after him. There was no response. She kept screaming as if the echoes were her only friends.

5

Filled with a stifling terror that had built upon itself over the years, Sally Ann felt her way along the side of the tunnel toward the opening she had first come through so long ago. Still sobbing and aching for her runaway son, she had but one thing in mind—to show him the truth. How could he not believe her? When she stopped to rest there was only silence around her. She heard nothing of her son but did not worry. Clint was far more capable of navigating the winding tunnels than she. She also resisted the temptation of calling Jackie. This was a situation she would have to deal with on her own.

For the first time, doubts began to fill her mind. Maybe it was all a lie. Maybe Jackie was a lie, too. Maybe this was all a dream, a nightmare; maybe there was nothing, really, except her and the darkness. No caves, no tunnels, no Clint, no Michael, no God. Maybe she was the product of the imagination of some madman who was dreaming. Maybe she was the central character of a novel, and the imagery of the writer was strong enough to flash her into existence. How else could she explain Jackie? Was he just the product of her need? How could he be real?

"There is only one way to find out. I will prove to Clint and I will prove to myself that there is something else—something better for us than the darkness, than these damned tunnels. I will get out of here and come back for Clint." She spoke loudly, boldly, as much to calm herself as in the hope that Clint could hear her.

She continued through the tunnel, reliving the journey from the tunnel entrance to the main cavern. She walked with her eyes closed, hoping her feet would remember the way and not let her mind guide her down the wrong tunnel, take the wrong turn at a fork, sabotage her freedom. When she was tired she slept, and when she was hungry she ate until all she had brought with her was gone. Still she walked, the ache within her abdomen a constant companion, the pain of a mother falsely accused of being dishonest with her child.

The old tennis shoes were finally rotting away, and she discarded the soles and the few strings that still held them together and continued barefoot. She soaked her cut and bleeding feet at the first stream she crossed.

There she found more food, and rested until she was able to continue.

Limping, stumbling, and near the end of her endurance, she sensed a wall in front of her, and made her way to it. It was made of bricks! The first manmade substance she had known since leaving the stairs. Clint would have to believe her now! She felt her way along the wall and finally, hands pulling on her hair, sank to her knees. It was a dead end. The wall was solid.

She rested awhile, then scavenged the tunnel floor on all fours until she found a pointed rock. Chipping away at the old mortar proved to be a tremendous task, but she kept at it consistently, resting when she was too tired to go on, and taking trips back to the stream for fresh food and water. There was no sound except her own raspy breathing, no word from Clint. She knew that she was quite lost in the underground maze, that her bearings were so far off she might never again find either the Home Cavern or the stairs. This wall was her only hope. There must be something behind it.

She worked at the cement, chipping an inch at a time, until she had loosened one whole brick. With bleeding fingers she worked the brick loose from its slot and pulled it out. Half fearing what she would find, she reached her hand in the hole and felt ... more bricks. A double wall. Her soul wilted. Would she never get used to disappointment? She summoned courage and patience and kept going. Eventually she had worked an opening that was five bricks wide and seven bricks high. She began scraping at the mortar of the inner wall.

The second wall of bricks was not as solid, and by putting her foot in the opening and bracing her back, she could make the whole structure give a bit as she pushed.

She worked one brick until it became loose. She

pushed it with her hand, then her foot, until it gave way and fell in. Holding her breath, she listened. Nothing. Then a splash, way, way below, and the nauseating stench of mold, must, and rotting stuff wafted through the hole.

It was an old well, and where there was a well, there was access from above. Overcoming her sickness, she doubled her efforts to push out the inner wall. With one brick gone, the wall crumbled fairly easily. Soon she had an opening big enough to crawl through.

The effort was exhausting. She sat back and rested while her mind raced ahead. Here is a way out for all of us! She thought of Jackie, and called him. Instantly, he was there. He looked in the hole, and pulled his head back in revulsion. "This place is diseased. You can't crawl up there. The well has been closed up for years. I'm sure the top has been sealed."

"I can do it. I've got to get Clint out of here."

"You *can't* do it. Look at you. You're skin and bones and half dead. Do you know how you'd get up there, with no rope? And once you got to the top, then what? How are you going to open the lid? Forget it, Sally Ann."

"I *can* do it and I *will* do it and I don't need you telling me I can't. Now you can help me or you can go away."

"I won't help you kill yourself. How fast have you been losing your teeth?" Her hand went to her mouth, to the sore gums and the holes she tried not to think about. "Come on, we can find our way back to the home cavern."

"And do what? Rot? Have you ever thought what will happen to Clint after I get old and die? No, Jackie, this is our only way out."

"What's the difference, Sally Ann? You can die here, or you can die in that hole."

She took his arm and looked into his eyes. He looked so sad. "Jackie, we can get out of here. All of us . . ."

"Not me, Sally Ann. I can't go. I don't know why, but when you don't need me anymore, I think I'm going away."

"Well, I certainly don't need you now!" She was instantly sorry she had said that, and had time only to see the hurt flash through Jackie's eyes before he faded away. "Jackie? Come back. I do need you. . . . Jackie!" But he was gone. She curled up in the corner by her pile of bricks and cried herself to sleep.

6

She took her time preparing for the journey. A plan was carefully followed and executed. She was determined to succeed. She began by eating all she could find. Each time she ate, she stuffed herself until repelled by the thought of another bite. She licked salt from the wall until tears came to her eyes, ignoring the stinging in her mouth, then drank her fill from the fresh water in the stream. She even fearlessly fished for crayfish, and ate them eagerly. She continually called out for Clint to come join her, but there was never a reply. She didn't venture out farther than the stream for fear of losing her way back to the well, but her voice carried, and was so loud to her ears that she was certain he heard her. Each time the echoes rang hollowly back to her, the ache in her stomach rang with them.

She slept on a bed of moss that her body heat eventually made dry enough to be pliable. She shredded it, braided it back together, and wove a bag that she could sling over her shoulder to carry supplies, but she couldn't make a rope strong enough to be of any use. She braided another bundle of moss to weave a kind of shirt, since her clothes were long gone and the air from the well was decidedly cool. She made a snug-fitting pair of booties and wound some more moss around her elbows and hands.

Finally, she took a deep breath and stood. She was ready. She grabbed a handful of pebbles and put her head through the wall. She threw a pebble to the opposite wall and found it to be only about three feet away. She threw a stone straight up, but could not tell by the sound whether it was bouncing off the lid or off the side. The stones fell a long way before they splashed. She pulled her head out of the opening and gave one last shout to Clint. "I'm going into the well now, Clint. I'll bring your dad back."

Feet first, she entered the hole and felt for the other side. The sharp bricks bruised and cut her ribs before her feet found a purchase on the opposite wall. She walked her toes down until she could slide her torso through the opening and rest her back just below the hole. Slowly, moving her feet sideways, then inching her back around, she revolved around the inside of the well so as to miss the opening on her climb up the shaft. Already she knew she was in for an endurance test the likes of which she had never encountered. Her straining back muscles screamed, and she rested, willing herself to relax, placing the weight on her straightened legs and her toes.

With her arms straight out to her sides, the weight of her whole body was on her toes and her back. She was able to give her back some relief by raising herself up on her hands a little. The rough surface of the well wall helped. She was afraid her shoulders or elbows might give way, though, so this was only a momentary respite.

Up and up, through the vertical tunnel that had no ending and no beginning, she focused her mind on freedom and light and laughter in the sunshine and willed her bruised and torn back to go just one more inch, then one more, and another after that. She ate from her store and rested often, afraid of falling asleep, afraid of not falling asleep. Eventually she had blackout periods where she lost consciousness, and she was sure it was her mind insisting on the sleep she was denying it. Each time she awakened, her knees were locked tight and secure, but it was still startling, and her heart pounded.

Except for the loosened chunks of mortar and dirt splashing in the water far below, the only sound in the well was her echoed breathing. Now and then she heard a soft scuttling noise, but she refused to let her mind dwell on what might be making such a sound. She finally removed the moss shirt she had made when the moss became embedded in the lacerations on her back. This exertion was enough to make her pant for breath and stay still until the dizziness left her. She put what was left of the bloody moss into her bag and continued her ascent after her head had cleared.

Feeling faint and frail, she stopped and considered going back to the tunnel, but she wasn't sure how far she had come, nor was she sure how far she had to go. The blackness was absolute. Going down would be as bad as going up, she reasoned, so she might as well make for the top. Giving up would be the same either way. Archaeologists would either find her bones wedged in the well shaft like a prop, or they would find them at the bottom. She felt the rough brick biting into her shoulders as she continued, and whispered a little prayer that thundered in the silence. Time for a rest. Just a little sleep. She knew she was in danger of hallucinating from lack of sleep and that her mind wasn't functioning clearly, so she wedged herself in very tightly and planned to rest there for a while. Sleep came quickly.

When she awoke, there were insects crawling over her legs. She screamed and brushed at her legs with her shoulder bag. "Oh, God! Get them off of me!" Cockroaches. They were two inches long, attracted by the smell of the rotting slugs in her bag and the blood and raw flesh of her feet and back. At her violent movements they scurried away—to wait. She suppressed the bile rising in her throat, and knew that if she allowed herself to be surprised like that again, she would be likely to fall. Then the venomous little beasts could feast.

She began again her torturous climb. Below her she could hear scrapings, but dared not think about their significance. She had to concentrate. As she moved upward inch by agonizing inch, she felt close to losing all. This was a foolish venture, and now she would die and it would all be for nothing.

"Mommy?"

"Oh, Jesus." More of a groan than words, she cursed the obsession that kept Clint foremost in her mind. She was surely hallucinating.

"Mommy, are you up there?"

"Clint!" The cry came from the depths of her soul. "Clint. I'm going to get us out of here." As she spoke, her voice reverberated around the walls of her circular cell, but she noticed a new dimension in the echoes, a flat sound from above. She was near the top! "Clint! I'm almost out! I'll come back and bring your daddy to get you out. Stay there."

The small voice came from far below. Much farther than she believed she could have come.

"Mommy, come back. Don't leave me here alone.

You don't need to go, Mommy. The darkness loves us."

Darkness? How could he talk of darkness? Pieces of thoughts, concepts swirled through her fevered brain. How could he talk of darkness when he knew nothing else? There is only darkness when there is light to compare it with. Does he believe, then? Exhausted, she could talk no longer. "Wait there for me, Clint."

She rested for a while before continuing. Knowing she was near the top gave her added strength, but even when the spirit is renewed, the flesh needs sustenance. She knew from the odor that the food in her bag was no longer edible. She ripped the moss armband from her elbow and chewed on it. She managed to swallow a couple of mouthfuls before continuing. She also knew she was losing a fair amount of blood. It mixed with her sweat and trickled down her back. She couldn't quit now. Her baby depended on her.

She persevered, eyes closed, up the wall which was growing continually warmer. She kept going until she heard her breath echo off the lid; then she raised her hands and felt it. Wooden. Old. Cracked in the middle and split along one side. She braced her poor toes against the far wall and pushed with one arm. The bricks ripped freshly into the skin on her shoulders, but the wood gave a little bit. Encouraged, and blinded to the pain by the relief she saw in store, she heaved with all she had. One leg slipped off the wall, and for one precious moment, one heart-stopping second, she hung suspended, held only by one toe and one shoulder. Holding her breath, she inched her other leg up to join the first one, the muscles groaning and stiff, and soon she again had both feet on the wall. The blood rushed through her veins with a maddening roar. She rested.

Try again, she encouraged herself. She found one crack with the tips of her fingers and felt its length, looking for an opening large enough to accommodate her hand. Almost, but not quite. The second crack was a little bit wider, and by sacrificing the skin from her knuckles, she could get her fingers all the way through. She pulled, then pushed, and felt, then heard, the old wood splinter. Carefully, so she would not lose her precarious balance, she wiggled the board back and forth until it came loose, and she dropped it to the water below.

The opening was now about four inches wide and a foot and a half long. She inched her way up and reached through the hole; she felt nothing. She loosened the next board and it came away more easily; now a full half of the opening was uncovered. The remaining half of the cover was loose, and she wrestled with it, afraid it would fall on her on its way past. Successful, she heard it bounce and scrape its way to the bottom, for a final splash. The opening was now clear. So why wasn't there fresh air to breathe?

PART TWO

I

Michael strode up the porch steps and into the kitchen, the screen door slamming behind him. He kissed his wife on the side of the neck, then pulled a cold beer from the refrigerator and sat at the kitchen table before opening it. She was a lovely girl, Maggie. A little plumper than the day they had married, but her face was just as pleasant and her disposition just as cheerful. She had passed that precious quality on to their children, too, both in their natural demeanor and in their attitudes. He loved her very much.

Maggie dried her hands on her apron, poured herself a glass of fresh lemonade, and sat at the table with him. The kids were not yet home from school, and these midafternoon talks with just the two of them at the kitchen table had become a daily ritual, one they both enjoyed. She looked at him closely. The years were wearing on him well. The lines etched deeply in his skin gave his face character. Tanned and rough, with a generous sprinkling of gray in his hair, he was more handsome now than ever before. Put a suit on him and he'd look the picture of a successful executive. She smiled. He was a farmer, though, and she liked that.

"I went to see your mom today," he said.

"How is she?" Michael had always felt closer to Maggie's parents than she had, and he visited Cora often since her husband had died of a stroke two years ago in the fields.

"She's good. She sent her love to you and the kids. She also sent some peaches she put up last season. They're in the truck."

Michael wished Maggie would pay more attention to her mother but didn't press the issue. He knew the problem. He sipped his beer.

Maggie stared into her glass. "I thought I'd drive her into town tomorrow. Maybe we could go shopping or something." Michael worked hard to suppress his surprise and pleasure. He didn't want to overdo it, but to have his wife and her mother together on a social basis was more than he could have wished for. It was, in fact, an answer to his prayers.

"I think that's a fine idea. Why don't you pick up some more yarn and knit me another of those sweaters? The winter is coming, and I've worn holes in the elbows of my favorite."

"What color would you like?"

"I don't know. Do you think red would make me sexy?"

She laughed and got up. "You don't need no help." She shooed him out of the kitchen and went back to fixing dinner.

2

"Momma? Sit down here a minute, would you, please? I've got something on my mind that I think needs put to rest." Maggie was in her mother's kitchen for the first time in a year. The table was piled high with their purchases from town, including some new red wool for Michael's sweater and a bolt of Pendleton blue plaid for the kids' winter clothes. She knew Michael would laugh when he saw she'd bought a whole bolt of it, like he did when she bought a whole bolt of red and white checkered cloth from the Sears, Roebuck catalog. But it had made a tablecloth, kitchen draperies, several aprons, towels, and dresses for the girls. He had liked the effect, even though it was all the same. Economy, she had told him, and he'd given her a kiss.

Cora sat across the table from her, a pot of steeping tea between them. She moved the packages aside and looked at her daughter.

"Yes, I believe it's time whatever is between us was laid to rest, Maggie." She poured the tea and waited.

"Momma, I've prayed long and hard about this, and I think I'm at fault. I'm feeling guilty, and have been laying it on you and Papa. Ever since Michael and I . . ."

"Hush, child. There's no reason to go over all that again."

"I can't hush, Momma. I've got to talk this out, and I've got to do it now, in order to cleanse myself and be rid of this feeling."

Cora sipped her tea and listened. Maggie always was a strong-willed girl. She waited.

"I guess I always thought it was wrong when Michael and me started loving one another, so soon after Sally Ann died. And then we went against Papa's wishes and yours and went ahead and lived together before she could be pronounced dead, and that bothered me a tremendous lot. That's why we went off and got married without you and Papa there. I was pregnant with Justin, and I was angry that we had to sneak around with our love for so long out of respect for Sally Ann's memory. When she just up and took off. Or whatever.

"But you have to know, Momma, it was all my doing.

Michael loves you as well as he loved his own folks, and he was against getting married without your blessings. But, Momma . . ." The tears began to spill over her eyelids. "I was so tired of having to deal with Sally Ann. I had to deal with her all my life, because she was older, and slimmer, and prettier, and she married Michael, and I was always so jealous. And then Michael loved me when she took off, and she didn't deserve him and I did, but still I had to live in her shadow for seven long years. It was hard, Momma, and it went against my grain, and I always felt you and Papa were disappointed in me for not respecting Sally Ann's memory like you taught me to." The tears were coming faster, and the sobs broke from her chest.

"I'm a good wife, Momma. And a good mother. Our kids are bright and nice and Michael and I love each other so much . . . and I love you too, Momma, and I want us to be friends."

She looked up and saw silent tears on Cora's face. Neither spoke for a long time. Maggie felt the knot in the pit of her stomach ease up for the first time in all these years, and love for her mother and sorrow for the missed chances in their relationship coursed through her. The pent-up flood of tears broke and she put her forehead on her arms and cried. Cora came around and sat beside her.

"Maggie. I know you're a good wife and mother. I've got eyes. So did your papa. And we could see the way you and Michael looked at each other. There are no more perfect grandchildren in the whole world than the ones you've given us. What happened with your sister is over and done with now. Only God knows her fate, and it was God that brought you and Michael together right here under our roof. We've always loved you, and always prayed that you'd come back to us. God bless you, child. You've lived with a burden that wasn't necessarily yours to bear. Come now. Drink your tea."

Maggie looked up and smiled at her mother. And soon they were both laughing. Laughing with a joy of togetherness that they had never known.

3

Life sure is good, Michael thought to himself as he loaded the last of the calves on the back of the truck. He jumped in the cab, started the engine, and with a final wave to Maggie, set off to the city, where the calves would bring a nice price on the auction block. He always enjoyed this yearly three-day trip away from the farm. It gave him some time to think, to miss the family, to see some new sights, to get a taste of the other side of life. It always renewed his appreciation for what he had.

As he turned onto the main highway, his thoughts automatically went to Sally Ann. His first trip to market was one week after she had left, and she was the topic of conversation all the way in and all the way home with his father-in-law. He never seemed to be able to drive this way without trying to figure out why she had left, or where she had gone. It was so long ago, but still the mystery remained. He couldn't bear to consider that she had been killed, or kidnapped. He preferred, no matter how much it hurt, to think she had left him and was living a happy and comfortable life.

Oh, Sally Ann, how I loved you. I hope you are well. With that, he turned his thoughts to the load of beef on the back of his truck.

Maggie watched the truck disappear down the highway and returned to the kitchen where tubs of plump blueberries were to capture her attention for the rest of the day. She got the recipe file from the shelf and pulled cards for jam, jelly, and Michael's favorite compote. She called to Justin to get out of bed and help her bring in the cases of jars from the barn, then rousted the twins to wash their hands, then wash the blueberries. Time they learned how to get their hands all purple, too.

She was holding the door for Justin as he brought in the last case of jars when the phone rang.

"Maggie?"

"Hello, Momma."

"Maggie, has Michael left for market yet?"

"About a half hour ago, why?"

"Well, there's a noise going on over here that's starting to concern me and I was hoping I could catch him before he left. I'd like to find out what's wrong. I sure hope it isn't the water heater again, but I'm afraid it is, and it's been going on for a couple of days now."

"Justin and I can come over before we start the blueberries, Momma."

"No . . . I hate to bother you."

"No bother, Momma. We'll be right over."

Maggie hung up and wished she hadn't volunteered. Most likely it wasn't anything they could do anything about anyway, but it might set her mother's mind at ease.

"C'mon, Justin. We're going over to Grandma's for a few minutes." The girls squealed with delight. "You two keep washing those blueberries. We won't be gone but a couple of minutes." They returned to their task with sullen faces.

Cora met them in the drive, and the three went behind the house to the water-heater shed.

"Now listen."

A faint tapping broke the stillness, erratic but high-pitched, metal on metal.

"The sound's comin' from over there," Justin said. They all turned to where he pointed, and saw nothing but the neighboring field and the old well cover that stuck up about two feet from the ground. Justin walked toward the well cover, but the sound had stopped.

"It was louder yesterday," Cora said. "I just can't for the life of me figure what it might be."

Justin stopped in front of the old well. "What's this, Grandma?"

"Just an old well, Justin. It went dry years ago and your Grandpa put that cover on it to keep you young'uns from falling in and killing yourselves. There isn't anything down there."

He walked over to it and knocked on the domed iron lid. It rang solid. A moment later, the tapping began, furiously.

"It *is* coming from here! Listen!" They all heard it.

Justin examined the bolts that held the lid on. "I'm going to get the crowbar and get this lid off here, Momma. There's something in there that wants out."

The two women looked at each other.

An hour later, the last bolt broke. Cora stepped back out of the way while Maggie went to help her son slide the heavy lid off the well. A putrid odor assaulted them as the top grated open. They stopped, caught their breaths, and gave a final heave, and the lid slid off the opening and one edge fell to the ground.

"Good God!" Justin's hand covered his mouth. Maggie screamed and backed away. A moan escaped Sally Ann's black and swollen lips as she tried to shield her blind, jerking eyes with a forearm that had lost its muscular control. "Momma, help me!" Justin shouted. Maggie shook her head, eyes riveted on the apparition from the well, and backed farther away. "Grandma?" Cora moved in quickly and, fighting the reaction from the terrible smell, grabbed the thin brittle wrist and stilled its flailing about.

"Grab her ankles, Justin, and we'll ease her out of there." Sally Ann had wedged herself into a niche four inches high by three inches deep, between the cover and the top lip of the well. Working carefully, pulling gently, one leg at a time, the hips, then the shoulders were eased out. They set her down on the grass and Cora sent Justin for a bucket of cool water.

It was the body of a little girl, but it was as light as a paper bag. Breasts were sunken into the ribs, and the toes were worn down, leaving raw wounds on her feet. Strands of blond hair remained, but most of the head was bald and raw, and her shoulder bones were laid bare where the flesh had been scraped off. Eyes were sunk deep into their sockets and as Cora washed away the blood and grime from her face, the girl became semiconscious and started sucking the cloth. "Easy, girl. Not too much to drink at first." She removed the cloth, and immediately the girl tried to speak.

The swollen tongue wagged through toothless gums as clicking noises came gagging from deep in her throat. Cora turned to Justin who was gaping at the sight. "Justin, get your mother and cover up this hole, then help me get this poor thing into the house."

Maggie stepped forward. "No!"

Cora turned and looked up at her, a puzzled frown asking the question.

"She's come back to haunt me, Momma. It's Sally Ann, back from the grave!"

Cora looked down at the frail creature and she caught her breath. "Great Mother of God," she breathed quietly. She scooped the girl up in her arms and carried her into the cool house, the bent baby spoon still dangling from one finger.

4

After a brief knock on the door, Cora entered the room. "Are you awake?"

"Yes."

"I brought you some breakfast."

"I'm not very hungry."

"If you don't eat, girl, you won't be able to keep up your strength." Cora set the tray down on the dresser. "Here. At least have some toast."

Sally Ann sat up in bed and took the plate of wheat toast from her mother. "Thanks."

"And after you eat, I'll take another look at those toes. You should be up and walking about now. That'll bring back your appetite."

"I want to see Michael."

Cora sighed. She drew up a chair from the desk and sat down. "I guess it's time we talked the truth to each other, Sally Ann. Michael doesn't know you're here."

"Well, tell him. I'm well enough to see him now."

"It isn't that simple. You see, when you disappeared, Michael mourned you for a long, long time. We all did. We didn't know if you'd run off or been kidnapped or what. But there was never any word, and so we finally had to get over it and get on with living our lives. I know your Papa prayed for you every day of his life. And Michael . . . well, he had to get on with his life, too. Once you were declared dead, he remarried. So now he has a family, and we don't want anything to interfere with his happiness."

"Any *thing*? You mean me! But if he waited so long, he can't have much of a family yet. Oh, Momma, the only thing that kept me going down there was thinking of Michael. I've really got to see him. I've got something to tell him."

"You've been gone a long time, Sally Ann. Michael and Maggie have four children . . ."

"Maggie? *Maggie*? Michael married Maggie?" Sally threw the covers off her legs and started to get up. "You've no right to keep me here. I want to see my husband."

Cora pushed her back to bed with one hand. Still so frail, she thought. "He's not your husband any longer, Sally Ann. He and Maggie have four children; did you hear me?"

Sally stopped struggling against her mother and lay her head back on the pillow. She closed her eyes, feeling faint from the exertion. She couldn't possibly have heard what she thought she heard.

"You've been gone twenty years, Sally Ann."

The room started spinning. She heard a voice from far off saying "Clinton! Wait for me, Clint." It was her own voice, but her head seemed stuffed with cotton. She felt a cool cloth on her forehead, and she waited until the buzzing in her ears died away. Twenty years. Twenty years of her life wasted in an underground hole. She was now thirty-six years old. And scarred and ugly and Michael was lost to her forever. Tears leaked out of the corners of her eyes and she reached for her mother's hand.

Cora was cleaning up the luncheon dishes in the kitchen while Sally Ann did her daily exercises on the living-room floor. Her body had healed well, and though the scarred skin was pulled taut over her back, the muscles were starting to come back. She had gained weight and walked with barely a trace of a limp. Her eyes had stopped that incessant jerking, and her sight was returning rapidly.

"Momma?"

"Yes, dear?"

The problem, as she viewed herself in the mirror, was the face. Her parchment skin showed blue veins as it clung to her bones. Over her sunken cheeks were patches of scaly skin that itched and turned red and white when she scratched them. Her head was still bald and scarred, even though the hair was growing back in spots. A scarf hid most of that. Her lips and what teeth were left were black as tar. She looked like a living skull.

She thought constantly of Clint—she missed him almost more than she could bear—but there were things she needed to do before she could go back to him. He would be all right. He was in his element, he was twenty years old, and—the darkness loved him.

"I want to go to town."

"I think that's a very good idea if you're feeling up to it."

"I want to see the dentist."

Cora stood in the doorway and dried her hands on a dish towel. Sally Ann looked up at her and said, "Don't worry. I'll use a fake name."

Pain crossed Cora's face, and she turned and went

back to the kitchen. It is so unfair, Sally thought. She was supposed to pick up the pieces of her life. But where was she to start, when her own family wouldn't even support her? Well, at least the situation was clear.

Cora walked to the bedroom and returned with a simple housedress that might fit Sally's slim frame. "Here. Try this on and I'll call Dr. Green for an appointment."

The trip to town was traumatic for both of them. Cora didn't like lying to the doctor, and there wasn't much he could do about Sally Ann's teeth anyway. He filled two cavities, gave her a prescription for vitamins and calcium, and tried to get her to come back for dentures. Sally Ann knew he was trying to be kind, and he was more than curious about her appearance. She thanked him and they were on their way.

She bought a new pair of jeans, tennis shoes, socks, several T-shirts, and a jacket. Clothes felt so binding. She also bought a child's sweater, size ten, light blue and soft. Cora asked no questions. The worst of the trip was the way everyone stared. Cora introduced her as a friend from the city who had come to recuperate in the good country air, and people were nice, but they still stared. They stared at her face, her teeth, at the way she walked, and they kept their distance. By the time Cora and Sally got home, both were exhausted.

The next day, the inevitable happened. After two months, Michael finally came over, to ask about Cora's friend visiting from the city. He had heard from someone at church, and was hoping to get some information about a man he was working with on a land deal. Cora told him her friend was resting, and she was, but she was listening from the bedroom.

Michael's voice. Deeper now, but just as she remembered it. Could it hurt him all that much to see her? All these years of thinking of him, dreaming of him, wondering how he was faring. What did he look like? What had twenty years done to his face? To his body? Their voices were a murmur now; she assumed they had walked into the kitchen to talk, in order not to disturb Cora's resting friend.

Then he laughed. A hearty, resonant laugh, and her chest constricted with brutal force. What has he to laugh about? When was the last time I laughed? Oh, God, I want to laugh with him. Touch him. She got up from bed and put on her jeans and a T-shirt. She wrapped a scarf about her head quickly and put the tennis shoes over the bandages on her feet. She looked in the mirror and her heart fell. I can never let him see me like this. She opened the door a crack and peeked out.

He was standing by the front door, ready to leave, when he saw the door open. "I believe your friend is awake, Mom. Do you think she'd mind talking to me for a minute?"

Cora paled as she saw the door ajar. "Well, no, I suppose not, Michael. Let me ask her." She walked over to the door, knocked, and went in. *"What do you think you are doing?"* she hissed.

"Why no, I'd be delighted," Sally Ann said loudly and pushed past her mother and out the door. She walked directly to Michael who winced as he saw her, then quickly recovered with a smile.

"How do you do? I'm Michael Hixson. I understand you're visiting from the city, and I thought you might know of a man by the name of Ralph Lederer. I'm thinking of buying a piece of property that he owns next to my farm and wondered if you had any word of his reputation."

He didn't recognize her. She was lost for words. She was ready for his hurt, his anger, his denial, his love, his passing out and falling on the floor, but she was *not* ready for this! What to do? Should she say, hello, Michael, I'm Sally Ann and we have a son who is living in underground caverns like a bat? Should she throw her arms around him and kiss him and make him forget all about Maggie? Should she embarrass him and say, Michael, don't you even recognize your own wife when you see her? Should she sink to the floor and hug his knees and say how long she'd been dreaming of this moment?

She stared at him, then looked at her feet. "I don't know, Mr. Hixson. The name is not familiar."

"Well, okay. I appreciate your time. You look a little pale. Maybe I shouldn't have disturbed your rest."

"No, it's quite all right. Please excuse me." She returned to her room, shut the door, then leaned heavily against it.

After Michael left, Cora came into the room quietly and sat on the edge of the bed. Sally Ann was strangely quiet. The experiences Sally had gone through had prepared her in some ways for things Cora couldn't even dream about. "How about some lunch?"

Sally kept her gaze steady on the ceiling. "That would be nice, Momma."

6

Clint sat on the moss mattress and picked at it while he thought. He missed his mother. His eyes were swollen from crying, and his grief had given way to anger.

"I don't care." The sound of his voice in the Home Cavern was hollow, but comforting. He knew she had made it; he had stayed by the hole in the wall and listened. He heard other voices, and the hole was invaded by a powerful monster, a presence that pierced his brain and knocked him back into the tunnel. It hurt his head. It was like a dream he had when he slept, where images danced around and said silly things and "looked" a funny way. He still didn't understand "look," but that's what his mommy said. He lay there, frightened, until he heard the grating of the lid again and the monster was gone.

There really was an "up there." He had known it all along. He pretended he didn't believe, because he didn't want her to go. He didn't want to go. He liked it here. There were things to play with and it was comfortable. Up there was strange, and he didn't much like the stories she told.

"Why would she go there? What's up there that she needs? We have everything here. Why would she want to leave me?" Tears of anger again seeped out of his eyes, and he reached down to stroke himself, his only comfort. "I'd like to punish her when she gets back. Oh, yes." The pleasure was intense. "I'd like to hurt her like she hurt me." Faster. "I'll hit her and pinch her and knock her down." He thought he would burst. *"And she'll beg me."* His orgasm was violent, his whole body stiffened with the release.

Afterward, he felt happy and free. He went for a swim.

Every so often, he returned to the hole in the wall by the square rocks. She was never there. He felt lonely, he missed her, but he never really felt alone. The air of the tunnels, the familiar feel of the rocks under his feet, the cold ponds and their inhabitants were his companions. When he felt sad, or angry, he would think he had chased her away. Then he would stroke himself and feel better again. It gave him intense pleasure until he learned that cutting the fish was better. That was even more intense. He tortured them while they were still alive, and they flopped and writhed and slowly died.

He took all these fish and bundled them up in moss and carried them past the tunnel that led to the square rock wall to a different cavern, a cavern with a little pond on one side and a huge lake on the other side. He dumped them in the lake, far away from where the stench would bother him. These fish were dirty; he could not eat them.

But mostly, he waited. He sat in the dark, blind eyes staring into nothingness, thinking about his mother, choosing not to think about the light and the world above. He thought she would be back soon, and they would live forever in the caves. Together.

7

Sally diligently worked her body until it was fit. She swam in the old swimming hole she and Jackie used to frequent when they were children. She couldn't comprehend that she was now middle-aged, that Clint was twenty years old, that her life was thoroughly destroyed. She took long walks through the woods and the fields. The aged and worn boards that covered the stairs to the tunnel were still there, the lock and hinges rusted solid. She would sit with her back to the big trees and stare at the cover, thinking about time, about life, about fairness.

She'd seen Michael's children, too. Justin, about thirteen years old, strong, tall, looking much like his father. The twins, eleven years old, with thick red hair like Maggie's, turned-up noses and freckles; Ellen and Elsie. And Mary. Different from the rest. No more than four, she was small, thin, with hands and feet too big for her size and very, very shy. The children would swim in the pond as she watched, quietly hidden in the woods. She didn't want to frighten them, and she didn't want to have to answer any questions.

Cora was a good woman. They talked sometimes far into the night. But she could never understand. Sally Ann hadn't told her about Clint, because this was not his world. He didn't believe in it, and who was she to keep telling him that there was something better? She had survived with the dream that back with her family she would be happy again. She wanted a normal life for him. She wanted him to be surrounded by love and family and all the things she wanted for herself. But maybe none of that was to be for them. There was no happiness up here.

Her body was healed. She was gaining weight. Now she had some decisions to make.

Her mother encouraged her to get out and socialize, but the thought was frightening. She had nothing to say to anyone. Except Michael. She had plenty to say to him, and Maggie as well. But she wouldn't. There was no point. She sighed.

On the way back to the house, she saw Michael and Maggie's home on the hill where once her dream house was to have stood. The sun was going down and lights were on. It looked so homey, so comfortable. As if they had a will of their own, her feet took her closer to the house. She saw the barn off to the side. Michael kept it all painted up nice. The tractor looked fairly new; the grounds were neat, the trees tall and picturesque. Close enough now to see through the window, Sally Ann kept the big tree in the front yard between her and the kitchen window. When she reached it, she leaned against it and tried to talk sense into herself. "What are you hoping to accomplish by spying on them?" Her conscience would not let her alone.

The temptation however, ruled her actions, and she peered around the tree and into the kitchen. There was Maggie. Fat as always. She didn't want to see any more, but she couldn't help herself. She stood next to the tree, eyes riveted on the warm little scene inside, and she was fantasizing that she was the one in there, making dinner for the babies and loving them all. She was so caught up that she didn't hear Michael come up behind her until he spoke.

"Hello?"

Her face burned a bright red, and she was grateful for the fading light. "Oh, hello. I was, uh, just admiring your house."

He looked at her carefully. "You're Cora's friend, aren't you?"

"Yes. I was just out walking."

"It's getting late. I think you should be getting back." His face softened. "Can I give you a lift?"

"Oh, well . . ." She smiled. "If it wouldn't be too much of an inconvenience. I am rather tired."

"Not at all. Why don't you come in and meet my wife while I get the keys to the truck."

Sally Ann smiled inwardly. She felt devilish. She followed him to the door.

"Maggie? Honey, come meet a friend of your mom's. She was out walking and got a little too tired, so I'm going to give her a lift back." He turned to Sally. "I'll be back in a minute." He disappeared down the hall.

Maggie walked warily into the living room. Her tone was venomous. *"What in the hell are you doing here?"*

Sally Ann smiled. "Well, hello, Maggie. It's been a long time, hasn't it? You're looking well."

62

"Don't play cutsie with me, Sally Ann. If you tell Michael who you are, I'll finish ruining your ugly face."

Sally took a step toward her sister. "Maggie. I don't want to hurt anybody. I just want to make a life for myself."

"Then go make it somewhere else. You can't do it here, and you can't do it with us!" Maggie almost spit those last words, then turned on her heel and went back to the kitchen. Sally Ann sat down, put her face in her hands, and started to cry.

She felt Michael's hand on her shoulder. "Are you all right, Mrs ... Mrs ... uh, I don't even know your name—I'm sorry."

"SALLY ANN HIXSON!" she wanted to scream in his face. She looked up at the concern in his face and started to cry harder. "Can't ..."

"Mrs. Cant? Maggie? Would you fetch a glass of water for Mrs. Cant, please?"

Sally Ann took the proffered glass of water and drank it down without looking at Maggie. She didn't need to see the hate that was written all over her face; she could feel it emanating from her whole being. "Thank you very much. I'm feeling better now. Maybe we'd better go."

She went straight to her room, past her mother sitting silently in the living room. The next morning she was gone.

8

"Clint? Clint, It's Mommy. I'm back." Sally Ann raced through the tunnel, holding tight to the wrist of the wailing child she was half dragging behind her. "Get up and walk or I'll leave you here!" The child cried louder, trying desperately to keep up, hiccuping fear. "Clint!"

Her sense of navigation came back in a rush. She knew exactly where she was going. The tunnels were her old friends. The smell, the roughness beneath her shoes, the blessed darkness, all meant she was home. And at home she would find peace.

She felt empathy for the child trailing behind her. The initial blindness was an awesome, frightening thing. They ran through the first tunnel that wound around, then approached the huge cavern with Monster Lake. She tried to hush up the girl before they entered, and succeeded in lowering her screams to a whimper. Sally tried to suppress the terrible constriction she felt in her stomach as they entered the cave. They crossed the path between the lakes as quickly and quietly as possible. As soon as they were back into the comfortable tunnels, they took off running again.

"Jackie?" But even as she called, she knew Jackie was gone forever. "Clint! Come see what Mommy has brought you." Out of breath, they slowed to a walk, and passed an auxiliary tunnel that had a dank and terrible smell to it. The well was at the end of this tunnel. She stopped and put her face up to Mary's. "Smell that? You must never, never go near this place. The whole under-world is yours to play in, but you must return to the Home Cavern as soon as you get near that smell."

"I don't want to play here. Please. I'm scared. I want to go home."

"This is home for you now, Mary."

After an exhausted sleep, Mary was slightly more docile, and she followed Sally Ann as long as they kept contact with their hands. How flexible the young are,

Sally thought. How adaptable. The sleep felt wonderful. She awoke refreshed and invigorated. Ready for a new day. It was so good to have your sleeping and eating regulated by the body rather than by the sun. She laughed and skipped along the main tunnel, teaching Mary how to quench her thirst by sucking the dripping water from the side of the tunnel.

Eventually, they reached Home Cavern, and Clint was there.

They hugged each other and cried together and she felt all over his whole body to make sure he was all right. Thin, perhaps, but that is the way of the underworld.

"I brought you some surprises, Clint. Some jam." She took the small jar out of her bag and handed it to him. She laughed at his puzzlement, took it back and opened it for him. He stuck his finger in and licked it.

"Ick. What's that taste?"

"Sugar, honey. You're supposed to like it."

"I don't like nothing from there."

"How about this?" and she handed him the sweater. "Here, I'll help you put it on."

"I don't much like this either." He kept running his hands over the soft wool. "What's making those noises?"

"That's your new sister, Mary. She's come to live with us and be your playmate."

"She doesn't sound so good."

"I was afraid like that when I first got here. Be nice to her. She'll learn the ways of our life soon."

Clint walked over to Mary. "Wanna swim?"

"I want to go home," she sniffed.

"She's dumb, Mommy."

"Give her time, honey."

While Mary slept, Sally Ann and Clint talked. He

wasn't interested in hearing much about the time she'd spent "in the sun," but she did tell him that some people would probably come into the tunnels to look for them. "Can we find a place to hide for a while, Clint?"

"Sure. I've found some places that nobody else could find."

Sally sensed a change in Clint. He seemed older. Distant. Maybe it was because she knew that he was twenty years old, instead of thinking he was only about eight. Maybe being on his own for a couple of months had matured him.

After sleep they started. They dumped the jam into the lake and filled the jar with food. That went into her bag along with the extra T-shirts she had brought and some moss. Mary was a problem, but Sally Ann had expected it and was prepared. Clint tried to emulate her patience, but it was hard for him. He was so swift in the tunnels.

Clint led them down a series of side tunnels that were barely big enough to crawl through in some places. Up and down they went, following his lead.

Finally, one tunnel came to a dead end at a lake and they had to swim underwater to find the opening on the other side. This was nearly an impossible task for Mary, but the fact that she was so small and light helped a lot; they virtually held her breath for her and pulled her under and through the tunnel entrance.

The other side was a perfect space. It was dry and warm, with a deep swimming hole in the middle, and a brisk stream running down one side. The new Home Cavern.

Sally set up housekeeping, making beds, preparing a toilet, continually keeping her ears open for invaders. They came, but she never heard them.

PART THREE

I

Sally Ann and Mary sat on the side of the swimming hole, their feet dangling in the water. The children were playing loudly in the pool, splashing and laughing. Clint was throwing them high into the air and they begged for turns over and over again. He was a good father.

"I'm going to go away for a while, Mary. I have some unfinished business to take care of."

Mary grabbed her hand. "Are you going up there? Can I go and take the boys? Can Clint go? Can we all go with you, Sally? Oh, please?"

"You know Clint and the children can never leave this place, Mary. And your place is here with them. This is your home now. I'll be back. I won't be gone long."

"I wish you wouldn't go."

"I know, dear. I'll be back before you miss me. Time passes quickly down here."

Clint had nothing to say when she told him. His silence spoke of his disapproval. She packed some gear and left without further discussion.

The door at the top of the stairs was open, as she expected. She knew Michael would leave it that way in case any of them cared to return. She spent two days at the bottom of the stairs, getting used to the light, then ventured up. It was hot.

How do I look now, she wondered. She skirted

the woods and made her way to her mother's house. Strengthening her resolve, she knocked on the kitchen door. Her mother looked dully out at her.

"You've come back."

"Yes. Momma."

"Well, come in and clean up."

Not exactly a rousing welcome, but about what she had expected. After all, she had kidnapped Michael's youngest daughter and given her a life in the caverns. Not an act to endear her to the family.

After she showered, she put on the clean housedress her mother had laid out. She examined herself in the mirror. Her face looked about the same. A few more lines around the mouth and eyes, maybe. Somehow she didn't feel nearly as monstrous as she had the last time she was here. The smell of bacon frying came through from the kitchen. She joined her mother, wordlessly set the table, then sat down and waited.

"How's Mary?"

"She's fine. She's happy, Momma."

Her mother turned with fury in her eyes. "Don't you dare talk of happiness to me. You. Living under the earth like a worm. Destroying all that Michael and Maggie had by taking their little girl like you did. You're Satan himself."

Sally Ann endured her mother's venom. She knew it had to come out sooner or later, and was glad Cora could get it off her chest so soon. She stood up and put her arms around her mother as she stood at the stove. She felt the silent sobs shake her frail frame. Her mother had grown old. Very old.

"Oh, Sally Ann, why have you come back again? Just when a hurt has healed, you come back to pick it open again. Why do you do that?"

"I've come to see Michael."

"I guess I knew that the moment I saw you at the door. Well, there's the phone. Get it over with."

The number was written on a list Cora kept on the wall. Sally dialed the number slowly, praying that Maggie wouldn't answer the phone. She did.

"Hello?"

"Hello, Maggie. This is Sally Ann. May I speak to Michael, please?"

The phone bounced on the floor, and Sally Ann visualized Maggie's open-mouthed shock. The idea gave her distinct pleasure.

"Hello? Hello, who's this?" Michael.

"Hello, Michael. This is Sally Ann. Would you come to breakfast at Mother's this morning?"

"Oh, my God . . ." the phone went dead.

Sally smiled, slowly hanging up the phone. "He'll be right over, Momma." Cora left the room. Sally heard the bedroom door close.

Michael pulled up to the front door in a cloud of dust, got out of the truck, and walked up the front steps. He paused for a deep breath, then opened the screen door and came in. "Sally Ann?"

"In the kitchen, Michael."

He came in and sat down at the kitchen table. He was visibly trying to keep himself under control. "Where's Mary, Sally Ann?"

She turned to look at him and he took in the black teeth, the scaly, thin skin, the ragged hair, and the arms so thin they were like little sticks. All his anger disappeared.

"I came back to tell you that you have three grandchildren." His mouth fell open and he stared at her. "Three beautiful children, Michael. They play in the water and laugh and love. And they don't believe in you."

A new type of anger held him to his seat. The thought of three children in caves. What kind of a monster was this woman? Then he thought of Mary. Sweet Mary. Like a flower. She survived down there? But . . . who was the father? He laughed. "You're insane, Sally. There's no children. There's just you and your twisted ways. I knew Mary. She was too fragile. She could never have survived down there."

"You're wrong, Michael, *I* survived. And your *son* survived." Shock froze his face.

"My son?"

"Yes. *Our* son. And now he and Mary have three children. I'm sorry I don't have pictures of them for you."

He jumped up and grabbed her skull and started to squeeze. He could feel her thin, brittle bones, and he just wanted to pop her head like a melon. "You monster! I'll kill you for this!" His rage was born of fear, and didn't last. His hands slipped from her head to rest on her shoulders, and he started to cry. She put a comforting hand on his face.

"It's not so bad, Michael. They're really very happy. It's a whole different type of existence down there, but it's not a bad life."

"We looked for you," he sobbed. "We searched for weeks. There are so damned many tunnels down there. We all got sick. We couldn't believe that anybody could live down there. Oh, Sally Ann." He sank to the floor and hugged her legs. "My soul ached to think you have been down there all those years. All those years I had given you up for dead. I locked you down there that day and didn't know it. And I've lived with that guilt ever since."

She stroked his hair. "It's okay, Michael. I thought it

wasn't, but it is now. Everything is all right. Our son is a good man, and he's a good father to the boys and a good husband to Mary."

"When Mary was missing and Maggie told me it was you staying here with Mom, I didn't believe her. I hit her. She makes me so angry sometimes. But I had to believe her when your Mom said the same thing, and the lock was broken off the door to the stairs. Our life hasn't been the same since." Sally Ann smiled slowly above his head. "How could you . . . ? How did you raise a child down there?"

"One has to do what one has to do, Michael. His name is Clinton."

"My God. Will you take me to see them?"

"Of course, Michael. You won't be able to really see them, it's too dark. But I'll take you to them, if you like."

Cora paled when Sally told her what had happened. "You can't take Michael down there!"

"I can and I will. Besides, he wants to go. He wants to see his son."

Cora looked at her in horror, then turned to her closet. She put on a jacket and scarf. "Where are you going, Momma?"

"To church."

2

Sally Ann laughed when she saw what Michael brought with him. A whole backpack, with sleeping bag, food, fresh clothes, and flashlights. "No flashlights," she said.

"I can't go down there without a flashlight."

"If you take a light, you go alone." He saw the resolve in her grotesque face. Reluctantly, he left them behind.

They descended. She breathed the familiar air of the main tunnel. Refreshing. She urged Michael to walk faster, but he was unaccustomed to walking in the dark so their progress was stumbling and slow. "At this rate, it will take us a month to get to them." He didn't think that was very funny, but Sally laughed. He was amazed at her ability to navigate.

When they reached Monster Lake, Sally told him of the beast that lived in the waters to the left of the path. They rested near the entrance, and when Sally made a meal of the slugs they found on the floor, Michael found this practice so revolting that he quite lost his appetite. She laughed at this, too. "You'll be eating them soon enough." He didn't believe that a monster lived in the lake and told her so. "Take a swim in there, then, if you don't believe." The thought of swimming in total darkness made his flesh crawl.

He found his backpack cumbersome, and Sally was quickly losing patience with his slow pace. In fact, she was not as thrilled to be with him as she had imagined she would be. He was foreign here. This was not his element. He didn't belong. Well, she would take him to see his children and grandchildren, and then he could go back.

They tiptoed through Monster Cavern, then resumed their normal slow pace. Sally found the temptation to leave him when he was sleeping deliciously irresistible. He would wake up and find himself alone. The panic in his voice as he shouted for her was comforting. Then she would return to him and he was so glad to have her back. At last she was needed. Clint had needed her, but that was different. This was Michael, the man she had needed

72

for a long, long time. And now he needed her. Not for companionship, but for basic survival. She loved it.

They stopped frequently and slept. She convinced him that there were tunnels too small to take the pack into, so he agreed to leave it, taking with him only his essentials—sandwiches. Along the way she told him stories of Clint and his growing up and what a delight he was. He shared with her stories of his children. Justin, he said, was in the air force, thinking about making a career of it. The twins had been modeling and making television ads for some time. He spoke of his marriage to Maggie, how it had come about, how her father had died, the relationship between Cora and Maggie. She encouraged him to talk; it made her realize how little she missed that world. In fact, she was glad she was back where she was comfortable.

As they passed the tunnel with the dank smell, she told him of her grueling trip up the well shaft, adding bits here and there about how much she had missed him. He was horrified. She was glad.

They reached the first Home Cavern and she showed him where she had given birth, where for twenty years they had had their home. He was beginning to have an appreciation for her strength, her courage. She could feel it, and he made little comments alluding to the fact that he had no idea . . . Of course he had no idea. What a fool he was. She impressed upon him the number of smaller tunnels, some dead ends, some leading to huge caverns with hundred-foot drop-offs, the dangers of wandering without knowing where you were going. He insisted he would stick close to her.

She felt a growing surge of power in this relationship. The tables had indeed turned and she was enjoying every minute of it. She toyed with the idea of just leaving him and letting him find for himself the overpowering fear. Let him discover his own inner strength, she told herself with contempt. It takes no balls to ride a tractor. Was this the man she had pined for during more than thirty years in the underworld? This was her God, this weak man who carried peanut-butter sandwiches with him and whined when she wasn't by his side when he awoke? She must have been insane.

They continued through tunnels barely large enough for Michael's muscular body, up and down shafts, eating when hungry, resting when tired. They finally reached the lake, and the underwater doorway to Home Cavern.

At the large lake, they camped. Michael didn't know that his children and grandchildren were so close, just on the other side of the wall. No sounds escaped the underwater entrance. Suddenly she didn't want Michael to see them. She wanted to keep him under her control. She realized that he might want to take her babies back with him, and that was out of the question. She prayed Clint or Mary or one of the boys wouldn't come out this way while they were there.

"Tell me, Michael. Does Maggie know you're with me?"

"Oh, yes. She didn't like it, but then she doesn't like much anymore. I didn't tell her about Clinton. I told her you were taking me to see Mary."

"I see." Sally Ann grinned in the darkness. A plan was taking form in her mind.

3

After sleeping three or four times, Michael was anxious to get under way. Sally Ann delayed their departure as long as she dared, then led him down a tunnel, far away from the Home Cavern where the children played. She remembered from long ago another cavern, much like the one Michael expected, and she took him there. It took them a long time. She doubled back down different tunnels, and frequently he would ask, "Didn't we come this way?," and she would laugh at him and call him foolish. She enjoyed the power she held over him. It was time he learned something.

Finally, they stopped just outside the cavern. Sally Ann talked to Michael in a low voice, as if the others could hear. "Michael. They're not used to anybody else, you know. Clinton doesn't even believe in you, so he won't let the boys believe in you, either. Mary has been here a long time, and she's not sure who to believe, so don't expect a major welcome. This is their territory, you know, and you're an intruder. They may even ignore you, or tell you to go away. But they're flexible. They'll get used to you."

How well he knew what an intruder he was. She had made him feel very uncomfortable since the beginning of this damned journey, and he was now sorry he had ever agreed to come. He was totally at her mercy, and he didn't like that at all. She seemed a little crazed. "I'll be all right. Let's go."

They turned the corner and Sally Ann went dancing into the cavern. "Clinton! We're home! Mary? Boys? Come see the surprise I've brought." Silence reverberated in the huge room.

"There's no one here, Sally."

"Oh, they're probably just busy. Or maybe they're hiding. They'll come back soon."

They sat down to wait. Sally fidgeted, as her mind raced. They didn't wait long. "Here they are, Michael."

She got up and ran to the back of the cavern. "Hello, Clint. And Mary. How are you? I told you I wouldn't be gone long. Come say hello to your daddy." Michael was silent at the entrance to the cavern.

"There's nobody here, Sally."

"Nonsense, Michael. Here they are, right here. Clint, Shake hands with your Dad. Mary, where are the boys? Oh, here they are. Hello, fellas. My, you've grown, just in the short time I've been away. Michael, meet little Jimmy and Jerry and this is Jonah. Aren't they sweet?" She worked hard to keep up the chatter in the empty cavern.

"Sally, stop it!" His voice echoed in the silence.

"Why, Michael? What's the matter?"

His breath stuck in his throat. She was insane. She talked such a good story that she had duped him into coming into this hellhole, and now he was stuck down here with a madwoman. He turned and darted down the tunnel.

"Michael, wait!" She could hardly suppress the giggles that seemed to have overtaken her. Whatever had gotten into her to do such a thing to him? She followed him out, her tennis shoes silent on the tunnel floor. "Michael," she called out musically to him. "You'll never make it out of here aloooone." She heard his footsteps echoing in the distance. She skipped along gaily behind him. She would be sure he wouldn't get lost. But a good scare never hurt anyone, either.

She was surprised at the way he circumvented her roundabout path. He seemed to know where he was going and didn't get lost in the maze of tunnels and tributaries. He crawled through the smaller tunnels with amazing speed, and this gave her great amusement. All the way back she teased and tantalized him with bits and pieces of her thoughts. Always out of reach, her voice echoed around him. He remained steadfastly silent.

When he stopped to sleep, she would sneak around him and wake him with great peals of echoing laughter, eerie in the pressing darkness. The low curses he muttered to himself tickled her even more. What had gotten into her that she would act this way? No matter. He was close to the stairs now. They passed the well tunnel and she hollered ahead to him, "Michael. Cockroaches almost ate me in there while I was coming to you. Doesn't that make you hungry, Michael? Have some slugs, Michael," and her insane giggles echoed through the night.

When he'd had enough, he stopped short and hid quietly in a turn of the tunnel. When she skipped past him, he reached out and grabbed her. "Sally Ann. Am I on the right way out of here?" She laughed. "Tell me." He shook her until she felt her eyes rattle in her head.

"Oh, Michael. Don't be a spoilsport. Of course you're on the right way. I wouldn't let my little baby, the love of my life, get lost in these dark, dirty tunnels, now, would I?" He threw her to the side and continued on, weak from hunger, heartsick and tired. He entered Monster Cavern. She followed, making monster noises, taunting him, wearing him down.

"Come here, Sally Ann." His voice was calm, quiet.

"No, You'll hurt me. You'll feed me to the monster."

"Don't be a petulant child. Come here. I want to talk to you." He was sitting on a rock at the edge of the lake. She heard him pick up a handful of pebbles and start throwing them into the water. They landed with little plops. "Sally Ann, I want you to come back with me. They have places for people who need help readjusting to a new environment. I'll pay for it, and you'll like it there. There's no reason for you to stay down here and . . ."

"And ROT?" She shouted in his ear, surprising him. He stood up quickly, and his foot slipped on the rock. Arms waving wildly, he couldn't regain his balance, and he fell backward into the water. Sally Ann sobered immediately and went to his aid, but she heard splashing and slapping sounds in the water and the old fear once again took over her mind. She crouched on the path and whimpered.

"Sally Ann . . ." he gasped. "Oh, God! Sally, help me. Something's caught my leg. Sally! Oh, please." There was silence while he ducked under the water. He surfaced with a splash. *"Sally!"* One last scream, then he was gone. The surface of the water continued to agitate, and the waves lapped at her shoes as she stood in the middle of the path, horrified. Then all was silent.

"Michael?" she called out softly. Silence. "Michael, don't play any games with me. Come out of there." She backed up, toward the entrance to the cave. "Michael?" A little louder, a little braver. "Oh, God, *Michael!*" She turned and ran.

4

Clint didn't need to be told what had happened. He read it in her face, in her body, as they felt each other in greeting. He knew that an era was dead, that he no longer needed to view the other world as a threat. It was over; she was his now, like Mary, like the boys. He felt her loss. It was, after all, what had sustained her all this time. She would get over it. She was a survivor. Like him.

The angry meanness that had consumed him soon

after his mother had gone vanished with her return. He lay on his bed of moss, the only one awake, and contemplated his growing empire. Mary was pregnant again, but it wasn't soon enough. He told her she had to have a girl.

He would build something here far superior to anything up there. He and his mother. She would help him.

She needed some time, he knew, to let the wound heal. Then they would go up there, together, and get what they needed. Two more girls should be enough. Young ones.

He turned over on his side and snuggled up to Mary's back. His hand felt the smooth swell of her baby. Yes. He smiled to himself. This baby girl and two more.

BEAUTY IS . . .

CHAPTER 1

Martha Mannes was forty-seven years old when her parents died. Her father died first, and she watched as her mother called Mr. Simmons who drove out from town and took her father away. So when her mother died, Martha left her in the bedroom and called Mr. Simmons. He held Martha's hand for a moment, looked at her carefully, and kissed her on her forehead; then he left with her mother in the back of his long black car.

Martha was alone.

It was hard to remember just what her parents looked like. There was an old picture on her father's desk, of a man, a woman, and a little girl. They looked vaguely familiar, so this was the woman she thought of when she thought of her mother.

After her mother had gone, Martha continued to do all the things she'd always done. She baked bread, she went to town for groceries, she fed the chickens and gathered the eggs. She set three places at the table, and cleared away two unused.

Sometimes she missed them, but most of the time she just missed all the things they used to do.

Father used to yell a lot. "Tell your retard to chop some wood and start stacking it," he'd say to her mother. Martha would see the stricken look on her mother's face and get up to chop wood. She didn't know why mother looked that way. Mother called her Martha; Father called her Retard.

As the years went by, she noticed that no one yelled at her anymore, so she stopped chopping wood, mowing the lawn, and canning peaches. She hated canning the peaches. But she made bread. It was good, squishing the dough, and the white all over her hands and wrists and the counter and the floor. She made bread until the refrigerator was full, and she piled it up on the counter until it turned black and musty. Then she fed it to the chickens. "Chickens gotta eat," she'd coo as she sprinkled the bread crumbs in front of their house.

She was never allowed in the barn, so when the terrible awful smell came from there, some people came and brought her things to eat while they burned the barn so she didn't have to think about it anymore.

Since Martha wasn't chopping so much wood and canning peaches and mowing the lawn, she had a lot of time to herself. She did a lot of wondering. She would stand in the wooden doorway to her little home and look out and wonder how the weeds got so high, and would they get as high as the roof. She never found out, though, because now and then a nice boy from town would bring his big machine and mow them down. She sat at the scrubbed table and fingered the wide glossy pink-white scars that ran all around her nose and wondered where they came from. She wondered where the sofa came from, and how come there were always baby chickens and what made the stove hot. And then she'd get dressed up and go to town and buy more yeast and flour and sometimes Mr. McRae, the shopkeeper, would give her a cookie or some other little treat.

When Martha was fifty-four, she put on one of her mother's dresses because hers didn't fit her anymore.

She looked in the mirror and thought she looked very familiar, just like her mother, so she sat down and put on powder from the little round flat thing with the cracked mirror, then tried lipstick. Her lips didn't match so good when she tried to rub them together like her mother used to do, and the lipstick smeared on one side. She took a tissue and started to rub it, and suddenly a little face looked back at her from the mirror. A younger face, with darker curls, a girl with a lump of a nose that hooked to the side, surrounded by fat red scars. The girl had traced the scars in lipstick and mother was removing it with a tissue and a scolding. Mother was crying, and Martha didn't understand. Then the vision was gone, and Martha went to town.

She went to the bank first, where they all knew her. She asked for twenty dollars and they gave it to her. The pretty girl in the window told her she looked nice, and Martha repeated it to her. "You look nice today," she said. She took her crisp bill and went over to the general store and bought what she always bought. Milk, yeast, flour, sugar, and root beer. The 4-H kept up a garden at her house which provided all the vegetables she wanted. Especially carrots. She loved to pull up the carrots, all warm from the sun, wipe the dirt off on her dress, and eat them.

Mr. McRae, pleasantly scrubbed and mostly bald in his white apron, was always smiling. "Good morning, Martha. How are you today?"

"Look nice," Martha said.

"Yes, you look very nice today. Do you want the usual?"

"Flour ..." Martha said, ticking off finger number one.

"Yes. Wait just a minute and I'll get it all for you."

Martha waited, looking at all the shiny jars with the colorful striped sticks inside. Mr. McRae returned with a sack full of groceries and set them on the counter.

"What do you do with all this flour, Martha?"

Her face screwed up in listening intensity. "Bake bread."

"Freshly baked bread, eh? Do you eat it all?" He glanced at her bulk.

"Chickens gotta eat."

"You feed the bread to the chickens?"

She looked at him blankly. "Chickens gotta eat."

He leaned over the counter closer to her. "I'll tell you what, Martha. I'll give you some real good food for the chickens, and you bring me the bread you bake, okay? And some fresh eggs?"

"You want bread?"

"Yes," he nodded. "I'll buy it from you."

"You want eggs?"

He nodded again.

She laughed, a rasp, horrible in its lack of practice, her poorly sewn-on nose crinkling redly. "I get bread. I get eggs."

"Good. Here." He put a small solid sack of chicken feed in with her groceries. "Feed this to your chickens, and bring me bread and eggs, okay?"

She picked up the sack and left without acknowledgment. Mr. McRae shook his head as she waddled out of the store.

Martha headed for home. A block away from the store, she had to go to the bathroom. She paused for a moment and thought about it, then turned and walked through the next door she came to.

Her eyes opened in amazement. She'd never seen a place like this before. There was a long bench, only it was too tall to be a bench; stools were in front of it. There were little square tables and red booths. Three men sat in one booth, cigarette smoke curling to the ceiling. Sparkling glasses and bottles covered the wall behind the man who stood on the other side of the bench. He smiled at her.

She hefted her sack and set it on the corner of the bar and said to him, "Bathroom."

"Follow me, Martha." The smiling man with the white apron like Mr. McRae took her to the back of the room and pointed at a door.

When she came out, the three men were sitting on the tall stools. They watched her approach with greedy enthusiasm. One of them stopped her with a big rough hand. "Can I buy you a drink, Martha?"

"Drink?" She looked up into the cold blue eyes. Each tooth of his fierce smile was rimmed in gold, and a toothpick protruded from the corner of his mouth.

"Yeah. You thirsty?" He turned and winked at his friends. The three of them looked at her, smiling expectantly.

She smiled her crooked smile, trying to understand. "Thirsty. Okay."

"Draw her a brew, Mike."

"Come on, guys, leave the lady alone."

The smile faded, the toothpick trembled. "She said she's thirsty, Mike. I'm buying."

The bartender leaned over the counter at Martha. He looked menacing, coming at her like that. "Wouldn't you rather have a soda, Martha?"

She cowered behind the one who cared about her thirst. "No," she said.

Mike set the tall mug of beer on the bar, while the one helped her up to a stool. She sipped the beer and made a face.

84

"You have to drink it fast, Martha," he said to her with a wink at his comrades. "Like this." He picked his beer up and chugged half of it down.

"Fast?"

"Um-hmmm."

She picked up the beer and drank three swallows before coughing and choking. The toothpick man patted her on the back.

"That's a good girl. Take a couple more swallows. It'll go down easier."

She did as she was told.

Mike watched all this with a wary eye. These guys were troublemakers. Poor old Martha, she didn't hurt anybody; she was just a poor lost soul. These guys got no right to get her drunk. When she had finished her beer, a white mustache rimming her smeared upper lip, he said to them, "Okay. You've had your fun. Now get out of here."

But Martha, with a new feeling growing inside of her, put her hands up to the bartender's face and simply said, "Stop." The bar was unearthly quiet, with just the ticking of the clock in the background, while she tried to concentrate, wrestling with this new feeling, a new concept. It was a new idea, it was just out of reach, please, where did it go? Her eyes started to bulge a little bit, and perspiration stood out on her powdered forehead as she worked so very hard to grasp that one thing, but like a fine wire, it had sprung from her mind. It was lost.

"Lost," she said, slumping a little.

"C'mon, Mike," said the one missing a front tooth. "She just needs a little fun. Retards are entitled."

"Retard?" Martha picked up her head and examined each of the faces. "Daddy?"

"Oh, Christ. Come on, Martha, maybe you better be getting on home."

She remembered. "Chickens gotta eat," she said.

Mike smiled and handed her the sack. She left the bar, her feet unsteady, strange thoughts confusing her as she walked home. She walked toward her tiny little house with weeds up to the windows and scrawny chickens picking at beetles. She felt the warm places where the man had touched her arm and then her back. She walked toward the faded memories of shame and disgust and tears and sorrow, and suddenly she remembered the thread of her thought. She let it come, let it find its own way through the crevices of her mind, tried not to block the path of new understanding, tried to remember her mother's words. "Just relax, honey. It'll come. Be patient."

There it was, but not an idea—an overpowering feeling, a flooding of emotion, of understanding. The companionship in the bar, the nice Mr. McRae offering to buy her bread. Her breath came in short gulps. She wanted more of it; she wanted more people, more talk, more laughter. But she couldn't. She couldn't keep up. She knew she couldn't. A hot, solitary tear of loneliness squeezed out the corner of her eye.

The moment passed. Martha swiped at the tear with the back of her hand as she trudged home. "Dust," she said to herself.

CHAPTER 2

Fern Cook and Harry Mannes were married on Fern's seventeenth birthday. Immediately after the intimate ceremony in Fern's white house on the tree-lined street, the newlyweds took the train to the farm Harry had inherited from his parents. They had died of flu while he was in school, and without the minor support money they sent every month, he was forced to drop out and return to Morgan, Illinois, and the farm of his childhood.

Morgan was a small place, a nowhere place, and Harry spent many hours walking the campus thinking about Morgan, the farm, and his parents. God, he didn't want to go back. More than once he lifted his fist to the sky and cursed, then begged God to give him something better. His parents had modest savings, and he could always sell the farm, but it was his home, his heritage. When the bitterness had passed, Harry thought realistically about his situation. He knew he had to go back. The farm was his parents' life; they wanted it to be his life. He knew, deep down, that it would be his life. His whole life. Once that was decided, he began to think of the realities of the farm, and of Morgan. And he decided he needed to take a wife back with him.

He began attending the local Congregational Church and saw Fern, a small, dark beauty with a songbird's voice. Listening to her solo in the church choir was as close to heaven as he would ever get, he thought. So he went to church twice, and asked her if he could come courting.

One month later they were married.

Fern and her parents were very taken with this good-looking young man who had just inherited a farm. Fern was a constant worry to her father—she was too good-looking and too available—so he promoted this courtship with all his heart. Fern could do worse. He was flattered that an educated, rich man like Harry would take such an interest in Fern, but when the train pulled out of the station and his daughter waved to him one last time, he saw her not as she was—a young bride, in love and happy—but as an old embittered woman who had lived too long and known too much tragedy and grief. This premonition shook him, and the tears ran down his face. Even as he stood there, his petite wife by his side, he waved back and grieved for his lost daughter and her lost life.

Fern loved the tickety-rock motion of the train, sneaking glances at her new husband, thrilled with the adventure of her life. The suddenness of this turn of events was overwhelming, but she'd half expected it. She'd always known something special was in store for her.

Daddy always called her his special little girl. She was, she knew it. She didn't know how yet, but there was a seed of something buried deep in the soil of her heart, something special, that no one else had. As she looked at Harry, his hair slicked back, wearing his one and only suit, she felt the stirrings in her breast, felt the gift of her specialness sprouting and taking root within the nourishment of newness, surprise, Harry, love.

The trip took longer than she had expected. By the time they pulled into a tiny station with a tinier sign that identified it as Morgan, Illinois, she was filthy and exhausted. Dust clung to the inside of her nostrils and behind her teeth. She felt not at all ready to meet Harry's hometown.

Harry helped her down from the train, then handed her the heavy cloth bags she was to carry to their home. They walked down the main street, each with two suitcases, stopping frequently to shake hands somberly with old friends. Harry seemed to know everyone; he ducked in and out of shops, systematically introducing her to every person they met in the two sweltering blocks of town. People offered their condolences on the death of his parents, their greetings, their pleasure at seeing Harry come back to run the farm. He gracefully declined offers to take them out there, much to Fern's disappointment, but Hiram McRae, who owned the general store, said he'd drop some things off for them later. Then they walked out of town and kept walking.

The bags were heavy banging against her legs, and it was hot and her clothes were stifling, but Fern would not complain. She would not start their marriage grumbling. They walked down the main street until it branched off in three directions, and Harry guided her down the rutted dirt road for another half mile, to their new home. Harry became a silent stranger as soon as they left the town of Morgan, but she respected his grief, both for his fallen dreams and for his dead parents. She could feel the memories of his childhood closing in on him with every step. She kept her mind busy dreaming of setting up housekeeping, of eating fresh fruit in the shade, of their children playing on the lawn. She tried hard not to think of her best clothes being ruined by perspiration stains, or their wedding night.

The road took a turn to the right, and there was the farm. It had been beautiful once. Fern could almost see the way it had been, when Harry was a child. The way it would be again. They would make it even better for their children.

For now, however, it was a shambling wreck. Harry had been away at school for three years, and it was clear the farm had been neglected the entire time. The house and barn needed painting, the weeds had overcome the yard and were taking over the buildings, the chicken coop had collapsed, and a rusted hulk of a car with no wheels leaned crazily on two blocks.

Fern heard Harry curse under his breath, but she wouldn't let anything spoil this, their first real day of marriage. It was too new, too special; there would never be another first day like this, not ever again. She consciously put a lilt in her walk. This was a project they could work on together, be proud of together, a lifetime work of making the farm beautiful, a happy place to be, a healthy place.

They walked up the sagging porch steps, through the torn screen door and into the house.

It was stark. The furniture was heavy, wooden, and unadorned. The big room housed both kitchen and living area, with a wood-burning stove and scarred enamel sink. Filthy curtains that had been red-checked hung in faded tatters above the sink; the cupboards were open and the dishes filled with dirt. Dingy sheets were spread over the sofa and the overstuffed chair. The place had a look of hot summertime in the dust bowl.

They carried their bags into the bedroom, where Harry immediately changed into overalls and a white T-shirt while Fern modestly turned her back. Fern unpacked the bags, hanging their clothes next to the ones in the closet, and put on a cool housedress. Without a word to each other, they went to work, Harry outside, Fern inside.

She discovered a rather pretty, though faded, green and pink floral print on the sofa and chair. Under another filthy, dusty sheet, the bedspread was a hand-sewn quilt in a starburst pattern of gold and brown calico. She changed the linen, dusted, swept, and washed dishes. She hummed to herself as she worked. Her new husband would be pleased with their life here. She would make it so.

At sundown, neighbors came over with fried chicken,

cold beer, and news of the neighborhood. Sam and Addie Smith lived on the next farm over. They'd taken all the livestock to their place when Harry's folks took sick, and were mighty glad to see him and his pretty little bride come home.

Harry and Sam went out on the porch after dinner for a beer and a smoke, while Addie and Fern cleaned up the dishes. Fern admired Addie's strong, plain hands, her generous size, and the way she wasted no motions in cleaning up after dinner. Fern felt young and small and inadequate next to this obviously capable woman.

When they had finished, they sat at the scrubbed wooden table with fresh coffee.

"So. Here you are. Now what?"

Fern was surprised by this directness. She was soon to learn that farm people are rarely anything but direct.

"Well, I don't know. It's all a bit overwhelming."

"This place has been going to seed since Harry left. It's going to take more than three years to put it back together again."

"We're young and strong. We can do it."

Addie eyed her skeptically, then looked down into her coffee.

"A farmer's wife doesn't have an easy life," she said. "There's never any money, and there's always too many kids. The tractor breaks and the best milking cow gets sick and corn prices go down. You have to really want to do this."

"I really want Harry."

"Well, good. I hope you can do it. Remember, we're just yonder. Sam and me have been doing this a lot of years; our kids are all grown now and gone away to better themselves. I know a few shortcuts, so just ask. In the meantime, I'll pick you up early tomorrow and we'll go into town to buy you some supplies. After that, you'll be walkin', I reckon, so make your trips short and frequent."

"I will. Thank you. I appreciate the help tomorrow. We are out of, of"—Fern gestured around the room—"everything!"

They laughed together, the big lady with the wide-open face and light blue eyes, and the young, slim, darker girl with fresh hope in her heart and panic in her soul.

That night, Fern and Harry made love for the first time, not very successfully. Their inept fumbling shamed Harry and he was reluctant to repeat his performance. As it turned out, this was a blessing in disguise, for Martha wasn't conceived for two years.

Harry drew out half of his parents' savings and bought a sewing machine for Fern and paint for the house and barn, had the tractor fixed and bought seed for the garden. Fern went to Addie's house to learn to sew, and made curtains and work clothes. Addie taught her how to make bread, how to cook breakfast for a farmer, and how to kill and cook chickens. Addie was a godsend.

Her days were filled with hard work—chopping wood, weeding with a scythe, cooking, cleaning, gardening, sewing, and working with the chickens and cows. She walked to town every second day, and walked to Addie's every day in between. She lost weight, began to look gaunt and bony, while Harry grew healthy and hardy and muscular and brown.

Addie fed her often and well, asked after her health, worried over her like a mother, but Fern adamantly said she felt fine, she was just getting used to things.

What she was getting used to, in fact, was her growing sexuality, her passion, her needs and desires. Her

Christian upbringing was confused along with the rest of her uprooted ideals, but the sight of Harry's hard sweat-slicked body made her weak in the knees, and she would work twice as hard to purge the vision from her mind.

At night, they would lie in bed and talk of the coming winter, and as his voice droned on in the darkness, she would stare at the nothingness above the bed and dream of making love on the wooden floor in front of the stove. She would touch him, lightly rubbing her fingers across his back, and she would ache between her legs, the way saliva glands hurt with the first taste of sweetness. Usually she stroked him like this until she heard his soft snoring; then she would curl into herself and wait for morning, sometimes sleeping, sometimes not.

At the commencement of winter, Fern's gift blossomed. And so did she.

They had worked hard all summer getting the farm ready for the cold weather. They had a late crop of vegetables, which were put up and safely stored in the underground pantry. The house and barn were freshly caulked and painted, hay was stockpiled, wood cut and stacked, stores of food set in.

The sky turned the color of the dusty roads on a Sunday afternoon, and after lunch Harry took her outside, wiped the sweat from his forehead, tipped his hat to the back of his head, and looked up. "Snow's gonna fly hard, Fern. Tonight. Tomorrow for sure."

Fern remembered waking up with an air of expectancy, looking out from her second-story bedroom and seeing the first snow quietly covering everything in sight. She smiled to herself, anticipating a welcome contrast from the dry summer, but a quick look at Harry's worried face slammed her back to the here and now. This would be no winter for carefree ice skating on the pond at the park. This was living with the weather as you live with the soil and the water. This was life-or-death weather. Though the day was still hot, she shivered, as if a premonition slithered up her spine but didn't quite make it to her mind.

"Gotta get the tractor bedded down," Harry was saying. "You going to town today?"

Fern noticed the wind picking up, swirling bits of this and that, stinging her ankles. She thought of her winter checklist, and the things that had yet to be done. "Yes. Oh, yes, I have lots of things to be done."

"Good. Go to Mac's store and see if he can send a boy out to help me this afternoon. I've got to get that tractor jacked up."

Fern took a sweater, grabbed her list, and went directly to town, walking quickly, head down against the rising wind, wasting no time. Mac's son, Dave, offered to drive her back and help Harry with the tractor. Gratefully, she completed all the shopping on her list, more than she could carry in three trips. She loaded it all into Dave's buckboard, and with a snap of the reins, they drove home, shielding their eyes from the blinding dust.

Dave helped unload her purchases before putting the horse in the barn. He worked quickly, taking worried glances at the charged sky. Fern's heart raced with excitement.

She put the groceries away, stacked fabric, yarn, and other winter projects, stored kerosene and fresh water jugs. The next item on her list was to stretch the lifeline.

She ran down the stairs to the fruit cellar, found the old rope coiled neatly on a meat hook. She put her shoulder into it and lifted it off the hook. Staggering under its weight, she climbed back up the stone steps. The wind was louder now, and suddenly cold, carrying pieces of trash and small bushes through the yard. She dumped the coils on the porch, hunted for the outside end of the rope, and threaded it through the iron eye that was screwed into the house.

Squinting against the particles of sand that stung her face and hands, she located the other end of the rope and began dragging the heavy line to the barn. Her dress whipped about her thighs and waist; her dark hair caught in her lips and tangled in her eyelashes. The world had turned reddish brown and gritty.

She threaded the end of the rope into its iron loop and pulled hard. She braced her foot on the side of the barn and pulled with all her might, sucking in sand that coated her tongue, but the heavy rope lifted only a few inches off the ground. It would have to do for now. She tied it as best she could and slipped into the barn carefully, so the wind wouldn't catch the door.

It was almost silent. The barn was warm and cozy, sealed tight against the airborne sandpaper. The animals were restless, but quiet in contrast to the whistling madness outside. She laid a reassuring hand on each flank as she passed. They smelled like old friends. Dave and Harry were kneeling in the other corner, heads under the rear axle of the tractor. Harry looked up as she came in.

"I can't get the rope very tight, the one from the house to the barn, Harry; you'll have to help me."

"Okay. Be right back, Dave." Harry got up and trotted toward her. "How is it outside?"

"I don't know. It's wild."

They slipped out the door together; Harry pulled his hat down over his eyes. The wind had risen even more than she had believed possible. "I'll get it," he shouted over the incredible noise. "Go on back to the house."

She ran to the house, the wind catching her lithe frame and almost knocking her over. She leaned into it to maintain her balance, dust filling her nostrils, blasting her legs and arms right through her sweater. She followed the rope as it slowly rose from the ground and was secured to the barn. This was the rope they would follow to the barn, to minister to the animals, in case of blizzard. In a whiteout, Harry explained, you can't see your hand in front of your face. Men get lost and freeze to death two steps away from their home porch. When he told her about the blizzards, Fern put the rope on her list of things to do. She wouldn't take a chance that it might be forgotten.

As she went up the steps, she heard a new noise in the wind, a high-pitched scream, and wondered what was tearing away. It was the scream of metal ripping, or a nail being forced from wood. She opened the storm door, holding on carefully so it wouldn't slam. She stepped into blessed peace and quiet. She put on the tea kettle, then patted the dust out of her clothes. Quietly, she waited for Harry and David, fidgeting, absently wondering where David would sleep tonight. Surely he couldn't go home in this weather.

Too soon, she heard the pounding of boots on the front porch, and went quickly to open the door. Harry stood there, torso bare, little drops of blood oozing from a hundred places on his arms and chest where the wind had driven sharp fragments of rock and bits of sand. Dave was leaning heavily on him, his face pale, his arm wrapped in a scarlet, dripping cloth.

"Jack broke. Dave's cut himself bad." He walked Dave over to the table and eased him down in a chair.

Fern had never seen so much blood. Her stomach

went sour, and bile came up to the back of her tongue. This is an emergency, Fern, she told herself. Now prove yourself to be a resourceful wife. She poured warm water from the kettle into a big bowl and set it on the table, along with a stack of freshly laundered kitchen towels.

Dave's eyes rolled back in his head, and his neck muscles gave out; he hung limply in the chair. Harry peeled Dave's blood-soaked shirt from his arm, and Fern gasped as she saw the flesh of his forearm laid wide open. Tendons hung, bone glistened, and an artery, like half a worm, pumped hot red blood into the wound. Instinctively, she reached out with both hands and squeezed the two sides together.

A calm washed over her like a flood of warm water. All the panic of the moment, the fear of the blood, the anticipation of the storm were gone. Her eyes closed, and she saw clearly a blue liquid start to flow through her, saw it come through the top of her head, sparkling with little golden flecks, and it swept easily, pleasantly, through her head, her neck, down her chest and through her arms to her hands. They felt warm with the sudden rush, yet cool with the freshening balm. In her mind's eye, she saw the cool blue, like an icy mint, surround the hot throbbing wound, and the fever was drawn out, the pain was soothed, the blue liquid melting into the tissues like butter on a fresh hot roll. The rent flesh merged together again, naturally, melding and flowing under the touch of her hands.

The flow of blue trickled, then stopped. Gradually, reality reentered her senses. She heard Harry's raspy breathing. She heard the wild wind rattling and shaking the house. She opened her eyes. She saw David's unconscious frame lolling in the chair. She moved her hands, and saw the long forearm covered with blood, and a thin red scar running down its length. She dipped a towel in the warm water and washed off the blood. The arm was pink and healthy looking.

She dared not look into Harry's face. She kept working, cleaning the blood away, frightened, trembling, not understanding. When the arm was clean, she indicated the couch. "Let's get him to the sofa." She looked up at Harry. He was staring, open-mouthed, at her. She didn't want him to look at her that way. "Come on, Harry."

Between them, they dragged David to the sofa and laid him down. Fern fetched a pillow for under his head. Then she covered him with a blanket and made two cups of tea. Her hands were shaking. She had to keep them busy.

She put the tea on the table, then sat down next to Harry. He was still staring.

"That arm was laid wide open."

She nodded. "I saw."

"It's a miracle."

She thought about that for a moment. "Yes," she said. "I guess it was."

CHAPTER 3

Martha kneaded the dough. She pushed and folded, pushed and folded, sprinkling flour in the sticky places. It was an automatic, easy rhythm. Her pudgy fingers knew the work by themselves. As she pushed, her body rocked forward, up on her toes. As she folded, she fell back flat on her heels. Pushed and folded, sprinkled more white flour, pushed some more.

Her mind wandered.

The chickens squawked and fought over the new food. She didn't think they would like it; it was just hard pieces of corn and seeds. Looked like rocks, too, in it. But they loved it. They just scratched and pecked and flapped.

Martha tried eating a little of it, but it was too hard to chew. How can the chickens chew it when they got no teeth? How come they like that better than the bread? Mr. McRae knows.

Martha's hands told her when the dough was ready. She greased up a big mixing bowl and plopped the dough in it, turning it once to oil the top. Then she put a clean kitchen towel over it and sat down to watch it rise.

Now she could think about the sparkling wall. All those pretty glasses lined up in front of the mirror. All those bottles with different-colored waters in them. The cool empty room. No, not empty. There were those men. And that funny feeling when her feet wouldn't go straight.

She thought about that drink in the bar only when she had time to sit down and concentrate. She knew there was more to it than she remembered. She knew there was more to it than she would ever even know. She didn't understand a lot of things. Most of all, she didn't understand the moments of clarity she had, when the whole world looked sharp, in focus, and her mind understood.

It was as if she lived her whole life under water—no, under oil. Greasy oil that coated her whole perception of things, but once in a while, her subconscious would break through the surface, take a roaring gasp of fresh air, and look around while the filmy sheets of grease ran down her eyes. And at those moments, understanding would rock her soul with great heaving sobs of newness.

Then she would slide under again, swimming in murky clouds of distortion.

Somewhere, though, those pieces of understanding were stored. She thought of them as little golden eggs— no, little fragile bubbles—with knowing stored inside, and they were stacked up in little triangular piles in some unused storeroom of her mind.

Martha gave the table a slap that stunned her hand. Now where did I get such a thought as that? What kind of an idea is that, anyway, bubbles in my head? Bubbles in my head all right. Bubbles in that drink they gave me.

She wanted to go back to that place with the shiny wall. She wanted to see the man with the apron, the one with the toothpick in his mouth, and the one without a tooth in front. She wanted to feel a part of something, a part of a friendly something.

Oh, I wish could understand.

Then a new thought came to her and her brow furrowed, her curly gray hair slid forward toward her eyebrows, her lips circled up, and her twisted lump of a nose wrinkled.

If understanding is in the bubbles, maybe I can pop one and catch it.

But the storeroom was guarded by a monster. She had seen it in her dreams, and as she thought of it now, its monstrous face snarled at her. Sharp teeth dripping with vicious saliva were bared; purple pink gums backed by wild yellow eyes showed its ferocity. It lunged straight at her eyes, rotten breath pushing her back in her chair.

She stood up quickly, startled, before her feet were under her, twisting her ankle, the pain driving the vision from her eyes. She bent over and rubbed it, automatically putting her trip to town off another day. She couldn't walk on this ankle.

A glance at the rising dough showed it had a long way to go yet, so she hobbled over to the sofa and lay down. She put her foot up on a pillow. Comfortable, she looked at the worn brocade pattern next to her head and began to pick at it. How does this go, she thought, picking absently, pulling apart the threads to see what was underneath. All thoughts of the bar and the people who inhabited it were gone, chased away.

Martha packed carefully for her trip to town. She put five loaves of bread in each brown paper sack and filled two more little sacks with eggs. She wanted Mr. McRae to be very happy with her.

She dressed in a special red-print dress, her going-to-town dress. She looked in the mirror, thought she looked a little different but she wasn't sure how, put on powder and lipstick, and brushed her hair back. That was it; her hair was too long. If the girl didn't come soon, maybe she could cut it herself. Mother had always told her to keep her hair short, then she could just wash it with a washcloth and not have to worry about more soaps and stuff. But now her hair hung in gray curls around her face. She put more powder on her nose.

She put one bag of eggs in each bread sack and lifted them carefully. They were light. She went out into the sunshine and the early morning cool and began walking.

There was no one in town. The streets were quiet and deserted. She could hear the chatter of birds in some distant tree. Mr. McRae's store was closed, so she sat down on the curb in front, one paper sack on each side, to wait.

Was it that first day? When her mother died, Mr. McRae gave her a folder of pretty pictures. Under each picture was a whole bunch of squares. He gave her a red crayon and told her every morning to get up and feed the chickens, then to mark a red X in the next square that had a big black number on it. When all the squares were full, he gave her a new one, with different pictures. He told her that he was never at the store on the days of the first square. She tried to remember. Did she mark the square this morning? Was it the first square? She couldn't remember.

She didn't know what to do. So she sat there, to wait for something to happen.

But it was just early, and soon traffic started to come into town, and then Mr. McRae opened the door to his store and saw her sitting there. He surprised her; she thought he'd come up the street. How did he get into the store if she didn't see him? Was he there all night? He came out and helped her up and carried her packages into the store. He had such a pleasant face.

"Martha! How nice to see you! Had you been waiting long?"

She tried to think how to answer him, but he went right on. "And you've brought me bread. And eggs! Wonderful. Let's take a look."

He pulled each loaf of bread out and slipped it into a plastic bag, twisted the end shut and wrapped a little green wire around it. "These loaves are beautiful! How many are there? Let's see ... ten." He handed her a small sack filled with plastic bags. "See how this is done? These green wires twist together like this." He showed her, then watched her bag and tie two loaves. "Put your bread in these as soon as they've cooled, okay?"

She nodded.

"And eggs. Oh, my, let's get you some cartons. Did your chickens like the new feed?"

Her eyes opened with enthusiasm. She bobbed her head and opened her mouth, but there were so many words, they all got stuck. She didn't know which to say first. "Cluck, peck," she said finally, in a rush of air.

"Cluck peck. Right. It's cluck peck food. I'll give you some more. Now. You've brought me ten loaves of bread; I'll buy them from you for fifty cents each. And twenty eggs. I usually buy eggs by the dozen but I'll pay you for two dozen today, at seventy-five cents; that comes to six dollars and fifty cents." He counted out the money on the counter.

Martha just looked at it. She gave *him* money at this store. The bank gave her money; then she gave it to Mr. McRae. He wasn't supposed to give her money.

"No," she said, uncertainly, and looked out the window at the new brick bank building across the street. She pointed at the bank, then slapped her fingertips on top of the money on the counter. "I go bank, they give me money, I come here, give you money, take flour home."

Mr. McRae understood immediately. This was too confusing for the poor woman. Now, what should we do? "Okay, Martha. I'll tell you what. You use this bread and these eggs to pay me for the things you buy here instead of with the money the bank gives you, okay?"

Her face clouded over in heavy thought.

"Do you need more flour?"

"Flour, yes."

"And the rest of the things you usually buy?"

"Yes. And soap. And cluck peck." She was proud of the name she made up.

He laughed. "Okay. You wait right here."

He brought the groceries to the counter, added the plastic bags and three empty egg cartons. "Now, Martha. Listen carefully." Mr. McRae waved aside a few customers who had come through the door, holding them off while he explained. "I sell you flour, yes?"

"Yes."

"And you go home and bake bread."

"Yes."

"Then you bring the bread here, and I will pay you for it with more flour and yeast and milk, okay?"

"Trade?"

"Trade. Exactly."

"*Okay!*" She smiled at him crookedly, understanding at last. "You want more?"

"As much as you can bring me."

"*Okay!*" She turned and smiled at the customers waiting in line. "Trade!" she said, grinning widely; then she took her sack and left the store.

She walked into the sunshine and the beginning heat of the day. She looked over to the bank, new and solid, on the corner. She should go talk to them. This was the first time she'd come to town without talking to them. She walked slowly down the street, conscious of the door coming up on her left, the door with the glass you couldn't see through, the door with the shiny wall inside. She wished she had to go to the bathroom, but she didn't, so she couldn't stop. She kept going.

When she got home, ankle swelling and sore, Priscilla was there, with her haircutting scissors and a pitcher of cold, fresh lemonade. Martha put her sack of purchases on the counter by the sink and sat down at the table, pulling Priscilla down into the next chair. Her expression was intense.

"Mr. McRae and I trade."

Priscilla's tiny little features looked calmly on this gross older woman. Cutting Martha's hair was a chore, but one she'd promised to her mother. Every month she would come and do Martha's hair. She tried to make it as pleasant as possible, but Martha was quite disgusting.

She was overdue, and the poor woman's hair hung almost to her eyes.

"Trade?"

Martha nodded hard, shaking her head of hair that was way too long. "I buy flour, take bread."

"Oh." Priscilla's eyes lit up in understanding. "You're trading with Mr. McRae. How nice. I've seen your bread, Martha. You make a lot of it." She looked at the clean, bare countertop. Oh, God, I hope she isn't taking him that moldy stuff.

"Good bread."

"I'm sure it is. Let's do your hair, okay? Then we can have some lemonade, okay?"

"*Okay!*"

Martha put her head into the tub, let her hair be shampooed, expert, practiced fingers massaging the scalp. It felt good; even in this awkward position, she tried to relax. Priscilla rubbed some sweet-smelling balm into her head afterward, then rinsed it with warm water. Martha sat still, out on the porch in the heavy wooden chair, watching the little curls fall into her lap as her hair was snipped short again, while Priscilla chatted on about nothing Martha could follow. Then she ran her fingers through Martha's new short locks, fluffing it, and took the towel from her neck to dust her off.

"All finished!"

They went inside for lemonade. Martha smacked her reddened lips. "Pris. Teach me this?" She pointed at the glass.

Priscilla was taken aback. Martha had never asked her for anything before. Not in all the years she'd been coming to cut her hair. "Sure. Come, I'll show you the lemon tree."

They walked outside through the weeds, Martha

moving more slowly, limping on her sore ankle, keeping her dress from catching all the burrs. Behind the littered concrete foundation that used to be the barn was a little green tree with plump yellow fruit.

"Pick the yellowest and the fattest, see?" Priscilla showed her. Martha lifted up her skirt and filled it, like a basket. She carried it with pride back to the house where Priscilla showed her how to cut and squeeze the lemons, mix the juice with sugar and water. "Easy, eh, Martha?"

"Easy. Yes." They grinned at each other, freckles scampering over Priscilla's pert and fresh nose. Martha felt her own numb, meaty outgrowth ringed by scars, and the laughter fled. She reached a finger out and touched Priscilla's face, ran her touch lightly over the bridge of her nose, feeling her own face with her other hand.

"Like that, huh? Maybe I'll will it to you."

"Will?"

Priscilla was instantly sorry she'd been so flip. "You know, *will*. Like it's yours when I die." She let Martha's fingers roam over her face.

"Pretty," she said softly, and tears flooded Priscilla's lower lids. This poor woman. This poor old, ugly, half-witted woman, so alone, so rejected, so talked about, so teased. When Priscilla was in grade school, the worst insult a child could give another was to call someone a "Martha." And here she was, sensitive, human, just trying to do what she could with what she had.

"You're pretty too, Martha," Priscilla said, with surprising truth. "You have beautiful, sensitive eyes." She put her arms around the large older woman and hugged her close. "I'll come back next week, okay? And maybe we can learn to do some other things besides bake bread and make lemonade. Maybe we can sew you a new dress ... or ... or something."

Martha pulled back from the embrace and pointed at the calendar on the wall. "Which square?"

Priscilla put her manicured forefinger on the next Sunday. "This square."

"I be here," Martha said with finality. She was so pleased. She had learned two new things today. She waved to Priscilla as she pulled out of the driveway in her little blue car, then sat down. She thought about the smooth feel of Priscilla's little pink nose; she thought about Mr. McRae and trading; she thought that it was pretty good that she understood, at last, that the squares were days, and that Priscilla would come back on one special day. She smiled to herself and hummed a little, and rubbed her ankle and waited for the days to go by.

CHAPTER 4

Harry sat astride a kitchen chair, resting his chin on his arms. He watched his wife at work, bent over the young girl on the sofa. The girl's hoarse breathing broke the silence in the room.

It was Christmas. They awoke early to see fresh snow atop the yard, the drift on the north side of the house now higher than the roof. The day was ringing clear, with a cloudless blue sky looking down proudly on all the whiteness it had left during the night. Fern made a big breakfast while Harry tended to the animals. After eating, within the ring of warmth from the iron kitchen stove, they opened their presents.

Colorful boxes from the townsfolk were piled high under their little tree, gifts of gratitude from the people Fern had helped. Harry had to chunk out a little freezer room in the ice alongside the cellar door for all the turkeys and roasts they'd been given in appreciation; they'd all have to be eaten before the thaw.

Fern oohed and aahed over the hand-embroidered tablecloths and matching napkins, the quilt, the kitchen towels and potholders. Harry opened sets of coffee cups and a hand-painted teapot, feeling mildly uncomfortable. *He* should be providing all these things, not the neighbors. Then he opened his present from Fern, a brown-plaid wool shirt, heavy and sturdy and warm. Fern had made it at Addie's. He hadn't a present wrapped for her, but he took her hands in his, looked into her eyes, and promised a new room to be built onto the house in the spring. A room she could use for her sewing, or whatever, until it became a nursery. Fern wept a little, so Harry got up and put on the teapot. He didn't like tears.

Now those hands that had fondled delicate lace only this morning were moving quickly over the small form on the sofa. Intense concentration deepened frown lines on her forehead. What was she feeling?

Tom and Mae Wilson had driven up shortly after noon, their little girl wrapped with blankets. Mae had been crying; her puffed face showed it. Tom's face looked old and tight, as he carried their only child, born late in their lives, into the house.

With just a glance at them, Fern wordlessly swept the presents and wrappings onto the floor and helped Tom lay the girl on the sofa. She unwrapped the homespun blanket as Harry pulled up chairs for the parents to sit on, then poured them each a cup of tea, putting a little shot of brandy in Tom's. Tom sipped, then winked at Harry with a weak but grateful smile.

Fern worked quickly and quietly as they watched. She looked older all of a sudden. These few months since Dave's accident had put wisdom in Fern's face.

She'd gained a little weight, plumping up her breasts and thighs; she no longer looked like a skinny little kid—she looked like a young woman, blooming, with even a touch of rose in her cheeks. Harry thought she was gorgeous.

When Harry saw her working like this, he was proud. He felt like a rooster, wanting to strut in front of his friends and neighbors, the people who'd watched him as a child and put up with his boyhood pranks. Now he'd grown, and brought a healer home to Morgan, Illinois, and he wanted the whole community to respect them.

He looked at her, hardly more than a girl herself, leaning over the child, and blood pulsed in his loins. He wanted to pick her up and carry her to their bedroom and make love to her all afternoon, slowly, tenderly. But he shoved this thought from his mind, because he knew that after the Wilsons left, their little girl healed, or nearly well, that Fern would intimidate him, being a far greater, more gifted person than he, and he would be embarrassed and shamed. Not only that, but their lovemaking was never slow and tender. It was fast and rough, his need suddenly all consuming, and then it was over and he was embarrassed and ashamed again.

He hated this.

Fern was talking quietly to the child. Her big eyes showed white in the red of her flushed face; perspiration stuck her bangs to her forehead like tissue paper. She nodded in response to Fern's murmured questions.

Fern stood up and turned to Tom. "Please carry her to the bedroom. I need her on the bed where I can get around her." Tom picked up his daughter and carried her in, laid her down on the brown and gold quilt, then went back to the kitchen. Fern closed the bedroom door.

She sat on the edge of the bed, left hand palm up in

her lap. She passed her right hand a couple of inches over the child, from her toes to the top of her head. She could feel the sickness. The throat and the stomach. She laid her hand on the throat, the skin hot to her touch, and closed her eyes. She saw the familiar glittering blue sweep through her upturned palm, streak across her chest and out her right hand into the throat, it was cool and comforting, like menthol ice cream, melting on contact and sinking into the reddened, swollen tissues.

When the flow of blue stopped, she moved her hand to the other infected area, the child's right side. She felt a corresponding ache in her own side. Ignoring it, she concentrated. She made her conscious mind like a black drumhead, stretched tight. Every thought, every noise made little thumping dents in the fabric, so she shut them out. Pure and black. Peaceful and undisturbed.

Soon she began to get a picture. She felt she was crawling inside the girl's skin, around the different organs. In front of her were a cluster of polyps, like grapes, black and unnatural amid the pink, red, and white glowing of healthy flesh.

She got down to her knees on the floor, eyes still closed, and put her left hand palm down on the floor. In her mind's eye, she punctured each grape with a huge hollow-pointed needle, and drained the vile liquid through the needle, up her arm, across her chest, and siphoned it into the floor through her other hand. One by one, the polyps collapsed. When the procedure was complete, she raised her left hand to the sky and a dry wind whistled through her body, into the child's, turned the residue to dust and blew it away.

She was finished. She opened her eyes, the ache in her side gone. She looked at the little girl's face, pale, eyes closed. Her forehead was cool. She covered her with the blanket and quietly left the room, shutting the door gently.

An air of solemn expectancy met her as she returned to the kitchen.

"She'll be fine."

Mae crossed herself and sank her chin onto her folded hands in prayer.

Fern poured herself a cup of tea and took a sliced fruitcake from the ice box. Her hands felt a little shaky. It was so strange. She had no idea what to do in these cases, but the process was instinctual, automatic, as if someone else was at the controls.

Mae lifted her eyes. "Bless you, Fern."

It wasn't me! Fern wanted to say. But something told her that these people needed to place their adoration somewhere. She could only accept their blessings and give thanks in her own way to the God of her own understanding. Later.

"It was your faith," Fern said gently, touching Mae's shoulder.

"She's been gettin' sicklier and sicklier since fall," Tom said. "Then yesterday she came down with this sore throat, and I guess she was pretty run-down, because it didn't look like she was going to be able to manage a simple little thing like this here sore throat. This morning she didn't even get up to open her presents."

"Well, she's going to be just fine. She's sleeping now. Let's let her rest for a while; then you take her on home. Keep her quiet for a few days and she should be back to normal."

"Thank God."

"Yes, thank God, not me."

This was just too much for Harry. He grabbed his coat off the peg by the door and slammed outside. He stomped down the squeaky new snow to the barn. Winters were boring. He'd cleaned the barn, fed the cows and horses and chickens, milked, gathered eggs, fixed what needed fixing, and he was bored.

Fern has all her friends, and her sewing and knitting and cooking and cleaning, and all her healing and shopping and more healing, and what have I got. Damn! I don't even have Fern. I don't know how to take care of a wife, not a gifted wife like her. We've been married less than a year, and she's brought in more food and more housewares than I have.

He sat on a bale of hay and looked at the snow melting off his boots. She's a good woman, loving and kind and helpful. I know it ain't no devil got a hold on her, it's got to be the Lord's work. How the hell do you make love to the Lord's chosen one? Didn't even give her a decent Christmas present.

He wandered around the barn, then grabbed a broom and started sweeping the already clean floor.

He was rearranging the gardening tools when he heard the barn door open.

"Harry?"

He turned. Her young face looked beautiful in the soft barn light. She was wrapped up warm in boots and a long wool skirt and coat she had made at Addie's.

"Harry, it's Christmas. And a beautiful day. Let's go for a walk."

He kept fiddling with the tools. He felt her touch, light on his arm.

"What's the matter, Harry? Did I do something?"

"No."

"Come on then."

"You go."

"I want to be with you."

"You want to be with me, but you're always with other people, healing and doing God knows what all."

"It's God's work I'm *doing,* Harry. I didn't ask for this. It's a gift. And you can't turn down a gift that God gives you."

"I know. I just feel, like, I don't know. I don't feel like much of a man."

She turned him toward her with a feather touch. "You're my man, Harry, and I love you. Can't you be pleased, excited, that we're together in this?" Her eyes were moist, her face pleading. "Can't you see the love-liness of this . . . this gift? This ability to help people and ease their suffering?"

"Of course I can, Fern. I just think nothing comes from nothing. Somewhere along the line we're going to have to pay our dues. We've got it too easy here. I myself think I'd rather work hard—long and constant, and learn about life as it goes on. This seems too much like a free ride. Something bad's going to happen and it's going to hurt."

She stepped toward him, putting her cheek against the sheepskin jacket. His arms automatically went around her, drew her in close. He kissed the top of her head.

"No, Harry. Life doesn't have to hurt. Life is good."

They held each other while the cows and horses shifted, scraping restlessly in their stalls. While the barn smell enveloped them in its warmness, deep in Fern's mind, a little voice said over and over to her, "He's right. He's right. Get ready."

CHAPTER 5

Martha leaned against the doorway and watched the red, orange, and yellow sunset streak across the horizon. Above, the clouds were puffy white, but to the east, they were already dark, night clouds. Her feet were swollen, her ankle throbbed, but she was reluctant to go back inside. The cool of the evening was coming, and it was just beautiful outside.

She dragged the heavy rocker out to the front porch and lowered her bulk into it. Then she wished she had brought a cold glass of lemonade with her. It was lovely out here—how come she never thought to do this before?

Because I'm learning, she thought. I have a friend, and now things are different.

Inside, the little house was filled with emptiness. Priscilla had gone, and with her went the gaiety of life, the smiles and joys of pleasure. The kitchen table was piled with packages, and a new television stood in the corner by the sofa, but all those things weren't fun without Priscilla.

Martha rocked and watched the chickens scurry toward their coop. She unlaced her shoes and took them off, feeling the fresh air on her hot and wrinkled toes.

Priscilla had been coming over a lot lately. They painted the living room last week, a cheery yellow. Today they went shopping. Priscilla explained to Martha that the bank held a whole lot of money for her, and that money was for spending. They went to the bank and Priscilla talked to the manager. Martha made an X on a little card, and when they left, with everybody staring at them, Martha had more money in her purse than she had ever seen before. And Priscilla said there was plenty more where that came from.

They drove, too fast, it seemed, to the new shopping mall just south of Morgan. They bought two new dresses for Martha, some wool slacks and sweaters, since winter was coming, a new coat they found on sale, and the new color television with a box to change the program from way across the room. They looked at new sofas and chairs and bedspreads and curtains. There were more electric gadgets than Martha had ever imagined, more colorful things, pretty golden statues, books and pictures and paintings and lots and lots of people and even more cars. A whole farmful of shining cars, windshields glaring in the sun.

Priscilla had told her she had enough money to throw out all her old furniture and buy new, so they looked and looked and Martha loved it all, but she loved what she had in the house best. She bought new towels, though, for the bathroom and kitchen, some underwear, and six new loaf pans.

There were some heavy bookends with little golden birds on them that Priscilla just loved, so Martha bought those, too, and gave them to her. Priscilla's eyes lit up, and she hugged her, right there in the middle of the store. Martha felt embarrassed, so she took the mirror out of her purse and worried over her nose.

They went in and out of shops all day long, Priscilla laughing at everything and Martha trying to keep up. She tried to understand, she tried not to think about her feet, she tried to enjoy everything as Priscilla did, but she just felt out of place.

Finally, they left, and drove home with the car filled with crinkling packages and fresh things. Priscilla helped bring the things inside; then she left, and all the joy went out of the day.

The sun sank down and the shadows grew. Martha felt a chill, so she left the rocker on the porch and hobbled inside. She turned on the television and lay down on the sofa. There was a man talking. His face was green. Idly, she wondered where the green people lived, and when she woke up, the house was dark and quiet, except for the white fuzzy buzzing on the screen.

Martha twisted the tube of flesh-colored makeup and looked in the mirror. Slowly, carefully, she traced the scars around her nose like Priscilla told her, like she did with the lipstick so long ago. With an awkward little finger, she tried to mush the line out—"Blend it, Martha"—so it didn't look worse than the scars. Nothing looked worse than the scars. They began between her eyes and ran down both sides of her nose to her lip, half an inch wide, shiny and smooth with ridges like little ladders. On the left side of her nose, the scar was jagged. She blended as best she could, then powdered her whole face. It looked better.

She turned toward the door, then back quickly to the mirror to see what she looked like at first glance. At first glance she looked like Martha, with a crooked lump of flesh tacked on to the middle of her face like a horned knob on a tree. She had hoped this stick makeup would give her a nose like Priscilla's. Smooth and pink with little brown dots across it. Small, with even little nostrils. Her nostrils were warped—one was large and round, one was dented and caved in on one side. She striped on red lipstick and put on one of her new dresses. She was going to find another friend today.

There was still lots of money in her purse. She walked

into town, ignoring the bite in her ankle, and walked directly to the bar. She opened the door and went inside, her mouth and throat parched from the walk and the anticipation.

The room was even more magic than she remembered. It was cool and dim, and empty, except for Mike, who sat on one of the stools, writing. He looked up with a surprised smile.

"Martha! How nice to see you!"

She smiled back. She was getting used to people since Priscilla had become her friend. She knew how to smile, and sometimes she could talk, knowing the right words, and sometimes they didn't all bunch up in her mind and clog her mouth.

"How would you like a drink?"

She nodded and climbed gently onto a stool.

"What would you like? Root beer? Coke?"

"Root beer."

He brought her a frosty mug, then came around and sat on a stool next to her. "You look very nice today."

"Thank you." She spoke slowly and clearly.

"Are you in town to do some shopping?"

Shopping! I know shopping! "No, went shopping already."

"Where are your packages?"

"No, no, before. With Pris. Bought television."

"A television? Gee, that's great. Keeps you company on the farm, eh?"

Martha thought about this. "No," she said.

"Pris took you shopping?"

She nodded.

"Who's Pris?"

Her brow furrowed. Who's Pris? She took her fingers and made scissors around her head.

"Oh, Priscilla. The hair stylist. I know her." Oh, God, Mike thought. Priscilla. Golddigger.

Martha smiled and nodded. She sipped her root beer.

Mike and Priscilla had gone to school together. They were the same age, thirty-two. Mike inherited the local tavern from his dad, and Priscilla went away to beauty school. She came back after years of bad rumors had circulated about her and got a job with Shirley's Hair Salon in town. She was a wild one, all right. Spent all her money here at Mike's, hustling. Mike sighed. Every town's got to have one, I guess. But this is no good, her taking advantage of Martha.

"Priscilla cuts your hair?"

"Yes."

"That's nice. She does a good job, doesn't she?"

Before she could answer, the door swung open and three young men walked in. They took stools at the bar and ordered beers. They wore Levi's and dirty T-shirts rolled up at the sleeve. The one next to her had heavy brown arms with large smooth muscles. Martha looked at them carefully, but when one looked back, she quickly sank her gaze into the foam on the top of her soda and kept it there.

"Martha?" It was the man next to her. She looked up slowly, shyly.

"It is you. Hi. Remember me? Leon. I cut your lawn."

It took a moment for Martha to understand what he said, she was so flustered that a stranger would talk to her. Then she remembered seeing the boy on the tractor, waving to her as he left. She always went inside when he came. But surely, it couldn't be this boy. The last time she had seen him he was young and skinny. And this boy was older; this was a man.

She smiled at last, lines of confusion leaving her fore-head. "Leon?"

"Yes, Leon. Let me buy you another drink."

"No. I buy. For all." She looked at Mike, then busied herself in her purse. She pulled out a wad of bills and handed them to Mike. All eyes at the bar looked in amazement. Mike took the wad of bills, picked out a five and gave the rest back to her.

"Hey, Martha," Leon said quietly. "You shouldn't carry money around like that. Someone's likely to steal your purse."

"Yeah, like me," one of the other boys said, then snorted a laugh. He was cut off short by hard glares. His face reddened.

"I'll tell you what. After we finish our drinks, I'll take you home, okay?"

Martha smiled. "*Okay!*" Another friend. She glowed inside. She looked at Mike. He smiled, relief flooding through him. Thank God. Leon's a good kid. Always helping out. Jesus, I don't want any trouble over this woman.

When Martha had slurped up the last of her root beer and wiped the mustache from her lip, smearing her lip-stick and exposing some of the scar, Leon left his friends and walked out into the afternoon sun with her. He held open the door of his old pickup truck parked at the curb and helped her inside.

They bounced their way to the farmhouse, truck squeaking and rattling. "Gee, I better get over here with my mower pretty soon, huh?"

"Yes," she said softly. "Weeds."

Leon killed the engine and jumped out, ran around and helped Martha down. He walked to the door with her. "You know, we could fix this place up a little bit."

He looked up at the sagging roof over the porch. "This needs shoring up." He bounced on his toes. "Porch is solid." He walked across and looked around the side. "Chicken coop looks pretty sad."

"Lemonade?"

"Sure, I'll have some lemonade."

They went into the cool interior and Leon sat in a kitchen chair while Martha filled two glasses.

"You know, it looked like you have enough money in your purse to fix the roof there by the porch and the chicken coop too. And the whole place needs painting. I'm looking for a job, and I'd sure like to help you out."

Martha didn't understand anything he said.

He moved a little closer to her and talked more slowly. "With money," he pointed at her purse.

"Money, yes."

"I fix roof and chicken house."

"Fix chicken house?"

"Yes."

"Okay." She handed him her purse. He opened it, took out the wad, and counted it. Over five hundred dollars! He took five twenties and rolled up the rest of it.

"I'm going to take a hundred and buy some materials. When the work is all finished, you can pay me for my time, okay?"

She just smiled at him. He put the bills in her hand. "I'm taking this." He held up the twenties. "You pay me more later."

"Yes. Okay."

Leon looked around the little house. "Let's find some place to hide the rest of this money. He looked at the cookie jar, a big fat bear sitting up. He took the wad from her slack hand and went to the counter, lifting up the bear's head. "The rest of the money is here, okay?"

Martha giggled. Money inside the bear. "*Okay!*"

Leon finished his lemonade. "I'm going now to buy supplies. I'll be back tomorrow."

"Back?"

He nodded.

"Which square?" She pointed at the calendar on the wall.

"Tomorrow."

"Next square."

"Yes." He stood up and looked down at her. She was really something. Slow, yes, but there was something else, nice, trusting, like a little puppy.

"You leaving?" She pushed her chair back and got up, came right over to him and hugged him hard. He felt a lot different from Priscilla. She was small and tiny, and Martha's arms went all the way around her. Leon was much taller, and his back was wide and strong. It surprised her how different he felt.

Leon stood there, unprepared. He looked down into the gray curls; then, helpless to move, he gave her a light hug back.

"Friends hug," she said. Priscilla had taught her that. Now he understood, and gave her a good squeeze. She was soft and mushy under his arms and against his chest. Not at all like the skinny girls he took to the drive-in movies. They were slim and bony and they slithered around a lot under his hot hands. Martha was a woman, plump, soft, and cuddly. He felt himself push against the inside of his jeans. Jesus, Leon, you adolescent punk. He released her and quickly went out the door, waving.

"See you tomorrow!" He backed around and drove off in a cloud.

Martha sat back down in her chair, her fingers automatically searching out the imperfections in her nose.

She thought of Leon, nice, tall boy. He felt good to hug, the place where his body touched hers still felt warm and tingly.

She smiled inside. A new friend, she thought. A whole new world was opening up right in front of her eyes. She'd spent her whole life here in this house with just her mother and father, and now she was finding that there were so many other things out there.

Suddenly she froze, as a vision of her mother, sitting in the next chair, swam up before her. Her dark eyes were piercing. She said, "Do not listen to what your father says about you, Martha. You are a very special child, and you must let those nasty things just slide right over you. He doesn't understand you like I do. You are very special, and some day other people will understand that." The image began breaking up, and Martha reached for it, calling her mother. Don't go away, come back, tell me, tell me. Her fingers clutched only dry air, but for a moment she really remembered what her mother looked like.

The vision made her sad. Special. Like Leon. He's special. Like Priscilla. She's special. And I'm special too. And she wished again she could understand, and felt it well up deep inside her, like gas, only it didn't hurt, it felt more like filling up, like something starting to come up from the very depths of her soul. She groped again for the room of understanding, that which would make her normal, could help her keep up with her new friends, and the snarling growl deafened her as yellow eyes and sharp canines lunged and snapped with threatening viciousness. Her mind shut down. She turned on the television.

As soon as Leon and Martha left the bar, the two boys

ordered another round of beers and slithered into the corner booth, out of the bartender's vision.

"Jeez-us! Did you see that wad of cash?" The words kind of whistled through the space where he was missing a front tooth.

The other boy looked at him. "Yeah."

"Maybe we ought to go pay her a visit tonight."

"Come on. She's just an old retarded lady."

"Do you know where she lives?"

"Sure. Everybody knows where Martha lives."

"Where?"

"First farm on the right out the north side of town. Hey, Leslie, you can't be serious."

"Serious as a heart attack, my friend. It was your idea, remember?"

"Shit, I was just kidding."

"I ain't." His steely eyes glinted in the dim light of the bar as he sipped his beer and stared into his fantasy.

CHAPTER 6

The daily routine of life became easier for Fern. As the months went by she spent less time with Addie, feeling more capable of handling things on her own. The seasons swept through her life, one by one, all exemplifying their own personalities. Winter was a mean ogre, dangerous and ugly, yet his reign was oddly cozy and comfortable as they rested during this respite from the sweltering summer. Spring was a baby bunny, soft and warm, but skittish, and able to dash into frantic motion in less than a heartbeat of time. Spring was clean. Then summer again, a paper queen of vivid reds, purples, and greens, fading in the sunlight, turning all the colors a sickly yellow while the paper itself became crisp and brittle. Autumn was a deer, beautiful and swift. And winter had come again.

Fern did her chores cheerfully, always busy, mind continually racing on a path of its own, far removed from the repetitive tasks at hand.

She dreamed of becoming a great healer, speaking of God and love to multitudes of people on a grassy knoll. She dreamed of waving her hand over a hospital and having all within healed in an instant. She dreamed of being visited personally by God and all his angels one day while she was baking bread or making jam.

Harry was a problem. No, not really a problem; they just lived with a totally different outlook on life. Harry believed in a vengeful God; Fern believed in a loving God. Their differences of opinion always resulted in the same argument.

"I'm going over to the Nielsens' after lunch today."

"Someone sick?"

"Nat. He's got a fever."

"And you're going to cure him."

"I'm going to do what I can."

"What if he's supposed to have a fever?"

"I've been given a gift, Harry. I'm supposed to use it."

"To change the world."

"Not to change the world, to ease the suffering."

"There's got to be suffering, Fern. It's the natural way of things. You take that away, and there won't be any joy."

"God doesn't want suffering."

"It's up to him to put it here or remove it."

"Well, and he put it here, and put me here to remove it."

"That's crazy talk."

"Harry, I don't understand. I don't understand why my hands heal people. Maybe it's so they'll take a closer look at God. But I really don't understand why you're so against it."

"Because it ain't right, Fern. It just ain't right. And the longer you do this, the more credit you take for it, the harder we're going to get it."

When Harry talked this way, a terrible look came across his face, his lips turned back into a kind of a grimacing smile, his eyes winced to slits and Fern's blood ran cold.

Eventually, Fern learned not to discuss it. The arguments made them both feel bad. Harry learned, too, and tried to accept his wife's preoccupation as a cross they had to bear. He delivered scathing looks her way whenever she went to visit someone sick, and he would moon around in a dark cloud of despair and a feeling of impending doom for the rest of the day and the night.

Their casual talk was only of farm things and news of the community, things without controversy.

The talk in the community centered on Fern. Details of her miraculous healings were told and retold until they were blown all out of proportion. People stepped out of her way in town—they viewed her with a mixture of fear and respect. They never hesitated to call on her, though, when in need.

When she and Harry went to town together, he scowled at the way everyone treated them. He would become angry and silent. Fern could almost hear his teeth grind. In his fondest dreams, he hoped he and Fern would be looked upon as good Christian folk, salt of the earth, pillars of the community, but instead, he felt he was some sort of freak, a specimen in a bottle, something interesting to look at.

But he kept it to himself as much as he could.

Fern had come to know most of the people in the community, had visited their homes, had held their babies. The vision of Fern riding in a buckboard became a standing symbol of good on its way to conquer evil.

Then the community had something new to talk about.

Doc Pearson was seen around the Mannes farm frequently in the spring. The quilting bees and church socials were filled with excited speculation. Once Doc's diagnosis was confirmed, he told his wife.

"Morning sickness."

Mrs. Pearson grabbed her shawl and went to the neighbors', and soon everybody knew. Fern was pregnant.

A hundred hands flew to work, making quilts, diapers, knitting booties and caps. Here was a way they could all show their appreciation to Fern without one of "those looks" from Harry. It was plain that Harry didn't think too much of Fern's work, and thought less of the gifts. But the baby . . . well, Harry couldn't say anything about that.

And what a child they would have! Fern with her small, dark looks and Harry, what a handsome boy. Their baby would be a perfect angel, happy and delightful, and it would bring Fern and Harry together in a new way.

The whole town of Morgan, Illinois, was pleased. This would be *their* baby.

As soon as her pregnancy began to show, Fern stayed at home. Visitors came daily, bringing little treats for her, and loads of advice. Eat this, drink that, don't think about bad things, stay away from loud noises. Do this, don't do that, here, let me help you, sit down, put your feet up. Fern gained weight. And more weight.

She laughed readily, enjoying the attention. Her healing work was reduced to a minimum, emergencies only, and the friction between her and Harry disappeared.

The doctor said the morning sickness was good—it meant the baby was well seated. But Harry worried. When the sickness passed, as Doc said it would, and the baby grew steadily and rapidly, Harry lost all his foreboding and looked forward to the birth with exuberant enthusiasm.

He built a cradle, and a crib. He painted the new room pink and blue, and the ladies all decorated it like a nursery.

Fern sat in the overstuffed chair and knit and grew larger. She waddled around the house, doing little more than cooking, and toward the end of her pregnancy, her feet swelled up, and she moved barely at all. She just sat and grew.

Christmas came and went. The baby's room was filled with toys and stuffed animals and quilts and blankets and clothes. Fern would wander through the room, fingering all the handmade things and she would feel surrounded with love, so grateful for all that she had been given. This new life in Morgan was stranger than anything she had ever imagined, but it was a good life. Long ago she had stopped grieving for the old days in the white house on the tree-lined street.

After Harry went to work, she would slip off the huge dress Addie had given her and stand naked in front of the mirror. She was amazed. Her thighs looked like hams, and her belly like a pumpkin. Her breasts were swollen, huge, and they sat atop her stomach. Itchy, sore red welts striped her sides. It was not pretty, but it was certainly fascinating.

And she, too, dreamed about the future of their child. Could every mother feel this way about her children?

She couldn't imagine that. Surely no child was as special as this one. Did her mother feel this way about her? Did Addie feel this way about her kids? How could she ever let them grow up and move away? This baby would grow up with the blessing of God. Surely it is a chosen child, born to one who has his direct healing powers. She would spread her fingers over her swollen stomach and feel the baby, an active child, and wonder would flow through her entire being.

The winter had been mild, with less than three feet of snow. Fern prayed the weather would hold until the baby came, to make it easy for the doctor and midwife to attend. They'd settled on names: Martha for a little girl, Harry Junior if it was a little boy. The time was close. Fern just waited.

The weather didn't. The most disastrous blizzard in anyone's memory hit the Midwest in early January. It swept up huge mountains of snow, covering the north side of all buildings. The weight of the wet snow collapsed structures and homes. Some people were killed in the collapse; others froze to death as they wandered outside afterward. Livestock froze, water pipes burst—the toll in Morgan was heavy. The storm raged, a complete whiteout for three days. On the second day, Martha was born.

This time, this morning in January, with the baby so close, Fern watched, helpless, back aching, as Harry went out the door, one hand tight on the lifeline stretched to the barn. She would wait, heart pounding, until she again heard footsteps on the porch. Of all there was to this life, she hated most his treks to the barn during a storm. She hated to see his brown coat disappear before he'd taken three steps. She knew it took a long time to see to the animals, break the ice in their troughs, feed them, shovel, sweep, and spread new hay. She had it timed in her head, but every time he walked out the door, time stretched. She had to consciously chant to herself, "Patience. Patience."

She picked up her knitting. A little yellow sweater hung from the needles. She would knit four inches before she would worry. Four inches. She took each stitch deliberately, resisted the temptation to measure after each row. Her needles were rhythmic, clicking in time to her heartbeat.

Before she finished four inches, she heard his heavy step on the porch. She exhaled mightily in relief; she didn't know she'd been barely breathing. Then a terrifying pain ripped through her back, her sides, scraping slowly, with jagged nails. It was so powerful, so overwhelming, it crushed the rest of the breath out. When it eased up, Harry was kneeling by the side of the chair, looking into her face with worried brow. She took some deep breaths, perspiration beading on her upper lip, and managed a smile.

"It's the baby."

"Now? There's no way I can get Doc."

"Don't worry, Harry. This takes a long time. Maybe the storm will clear." He helped her to their bed.

The wind howled outside, blowing snow so hard it sounded like sand rasping off a layer of wood. Fern listened to it quietly, taking strength from it between pains. Harry made her tea, fussed over her, worried himself into a frenzy, and paced, cursing. He hated this. This was something he had done to her, and he was sorry. He saddled up a horse in the barn, to keep ready in case the storm eased and he could ride to Addie's. Addie had experience in things like this. Addie could help.

Just before the white dusk turned to dark, the wind

stopped. Absolute silence outside made Fern's raspy breathing loud and terrible to his ears. The pains were frequent. He'd tied a rag to the headboard for her to hold, and as he walked into the room, she was pulling on it, perspiration rolling down her face and neck, moaning, cords and muscles standing out in her neck and arms in dramatic chiseled relief. He slid into his overcoat, and when the pain passed, he walked to the side of their bed.

"Storm broke, Fern. I'm going for Addie," he whispered softly.

"No. Harry, it's close. Stay here." Another pain gripped her, and he ran out of the house.

Addie grabbed a coat and swung up behind Harry. Sam said he'd saddle up a horse and be along presently. They rode urgently through the knee-high snow, only guessing where the road was. The wind began to pick up again as they neared the house. They heard the screams, both fearfully telling themselves it was a trick of the wind. It was no trick. Addie jumped off the horse and ran inside, dropping her coat on the kitchen floor. Harry dawdled in the barn, his heart racing, feeling helpless and useless.

Fern's knees were bent high, tenting the covers. She gripped the rag, her face and pillow soaked. A wail began deep inside, forcing its way through her exhausted body. Addie closed the door quickly and whipped off the covers. The bed was soaked with blood. The wail stopped abruptly as Fern's eyes bulged, a dark vein stood out in the middle of her forehead, and she gave a tremendous grunt, a push, and Addie saw the brown top of a head poke out, then recede back inside.

"Push, Fern, he's almost out!"

Fern pushed. She let go of the rag and gripped her

thighs with strong fingers. Addie watched as they dug deep into the flesh, little droplets of blood mixing with sweat and trickling down her thighs. Fern's back arched with the effort, oh, God, it was so awful, it was right there, why won't it come out, push, push, oh, God, PUSH!

The baby gushed out into Addie's waiting hands. Fern fell back against the pillows, her eyes rolling. Addie noted it was a girl, and laid the baby down on the sheet. She quickly ripped the hem of her dress and tied the umbilical cord.

"It's a girl, Fernie. A baby girl!" So announced, the child took a mighty breath and let out with a cry.

"A girl," Fern sighed, trying to smile.

Addie ran to the kitchen for a knife, signaled to Harry who had just come in. "A girl, Harry."

"A girl?" His face brightened. It was over, and they had a baby girl. Addie bustled back inside the bedroom, Harry following her. He was not prepared for the mess he saw. It made him sick to the stomach. He'd seen plenty of birthings—cattle, sheep, dogs and cats, but never so much blood. And this was from his wife!

Addie cut the cord, then lifted up the baby. "Look, Harry, a baby girl!"

They both looked, and Addie's arms went limp. She almost dropped the child.

"Oh my God," she breathed quietly.

"I knew it, I knew it. I *knew* it!" Harry's voice shook with emotion, with grief.

"Addie? Harry? Give me my baby." Fern leaned up weakly on an elbow, looking at their faces. Something was wrong. Oh, God, something was terribly wrong. "What is it?"

The two stood there, looking at the child crying and

waving its little arms and legs. They looked at each other, then at Fern. Addie's face was a mask of misery and pity; Harry's had that strange grimace of distaste drawing his lips away from his teeth. "Oh, God, *what's wrong?*"

CHAPTER 7

Doctor Withins knocked on the screen door, startling Martha out of a television-induced drowse.

She scrambled to her feet quickly as the doctor came in, smoothed down her housedress, and patted at her hair.

"Hello, Martha!" The doctor was a big burly man, a country doctor, with a wide-open face and big bear hugs for all his patients. Everyone in the community knew and relied on Doctor Withins; he was even known to help a horse or a cow in trouble. Martha was a regular on his list; he stopped by periodically to give her a checkup and make sure she was all right. "It's that time again."

"That time," Martha repeated, delighted. She'd always loved Doctor Withins.

"How are you feeling?"

"Good!" Martha's eyes lit up. "Baking bread for Mr. McRae, got television, making friends."

"Well! Isn't that nice. Come sit down here, loosen the buttons on your dress." He set his black bag on the table and withdrew a stethoscope. "Friends, huh? So you're getting out a little more?"

"Went shopping."

"That's good. Take a deep breath. Good. Another one. Okay, now cough. Again. Again. Good. How are your feet?"

Martha held up her swollen ankle. "Hurts."

"Yes, I can see that." He sat down in a kitchen chair with the foot in his lap and probed it gently. "You twisted it?"

Martha remembered standing up too fast, scared, startled at the snapping jaws of her mind. "Yes."

"Okay. I'm going to tape it up for you. He fished in his bag for an Ace bandage. "Watch how I do this now. End under your foot, wrap once around the foot to catch the edge, see? Now wrap around the ankle up to here—not too tight, just stretch it a little—then fasten with these little clips, see?"

Martha nodded.

"Okay, now listen, Martha, this is very important." He spoke slowly, deliberately. "If your toes get cold or turn blue, you take this bandage off right away, rub your foot for a while, then put the bandage back on looser, okay? If your toes turn blue, you've put the bandage on too tight."

She listened carefully, then nodded.

"Take it off when you take your bath, then put it back on again. Wear it until"—he stood up and pointed at the calendar—"here, okay?" He put a little mark on a square with his pen.

"Next Thursday," Martha said.

Doctor Withins turned around slowly and looked at her expectant face. "Why, that's right. You're learning a lot these days, aren't you?"

"Yes. New friends."

"Well, that's good. Now. One more thing before I go. I think you need to lose some weight. Your ankle will feel better and so will your knees. Do your knees hurt?"

Martha nodded.

"Lose some weight and it will be easier for you to walk into town."

"Lose weight."

"Yes. Don't eat so much bread and potatoes. More vegetables, chicken, meat."

"Okay."

He didn't need to repeat it. She was learning. Her mind was growing. Maybe she wasn't as retarded as everyone thought. Maybe being cooped up here with Fern and old Harry for so long had retarded her more than was necessary. He'd stop in again soon. This was very interesting.

They both heard the truck pull up in the drive. Doc went to the door and looked out in time to see a rusted pickup truck slide around in a cloud of dust, its headlights sweeping the field, then disappear down the long driveway, three pinprick taillights winking out around the corner.

"Were you expecting someone?"

"No."

"Must have had the wrong house." He turned back to Martha. "I'm going to come back and visit next week, okay?"

"Okay."

"Do you need anything?"

"No."

"Well, good. I'll be going, then. Take care of yourself, Martha. Remember. No more potatoes and bread."

"No more." Martha stood up. She reached around his neck and gave him a big hug. He hugged her back in surprise.

"Bye, now."

"Bye."

She stood on the front porch and watched him drive off in his van. Such a nice man.

* * *

"Shut up, you little asshole." The words whistled through the space where a front tooth should have been.

"Come on, Leslie. You don't really want to go there."

"Which driveway? This one?"

"Yes." Ned slumped down in the seat of the rattletrap pickup. He would give anything to be somewhere else. Anywhere.

They slid around the turn, throwing rocks and gravel behind them, Leslie gunning the engine and racing up the long drive. His belly was full of beer and his eyes had dollar signs in them. He was out to get some tonight. They drove around the corner and almost ran into the bronze van parked by the front door.

"Doctor Withins. Oh, shit, it's Doctor Withins' van! Let's get out of here!"

Leslie hit the brakes, cussing, spinning the wheel, sliding the truck around in a circle. His luck. Well, that was fine. He'd hit on her tomorrow night, and he'd leave this little wimp somewhere else. He lifted the capless quart of beer to his lips and drank deep. He looked at Ned out of the corner of his eye, cowering by the door. I should just dump that little fucker out on the turn, he thought. What a jerk. Instead, he turned toward town.

"Let's get some action."

Ned said a silent prayer of thanks.

Leon showed up bright and early the next morning, pickup filled with lumber and paint. Martha was feeding the chickens, watching them squawk and scratch at the hard earth, pecking at the little bits of seed she threw on the ground.

"Good morning!" he called, as he jumped out of the cab and grabbed a plank.

"Hello."

135

"I'm going to start on the chicken coop."

"Okay." He looked so smooth. He looked so young and energetic, long muscles sliding under his skin. She watched him unload, then went into the house and sat at the makeup table.

With nervous hands she worked meticulously on her nose, looking carefully from all angles. She powdered once, then again as an immediate shine crept through the heat and the powder. The lipstick was crayoned on next, and she smiled in the mirror. Leon would like her. He was going to be here for a lot of days. They would become good friends. She wished she had some of that light blue that Priscilla put on her eyelids. Next time she went to the store, she would get some.

Just before noon, she limped past the chicken coop where Leon was hammering and picked fresh lemons. She made a big pitcher of lemonade and a plate of tuna-fish sandwiches. Then she sat at the table, nervously picking at the hem of her dress, and waited.

She jumped when she heard his sneaker-light step on the porch; he swung open the screen door and came in.

His sweaty presence overpowered the room. He looked at the plate of sandwiches and glistening pitcher and smiled.

"Lunch. I'm starved!" He went to the kitchen sink, washed his hands, then ducked his head under the faucet. He came up dripping, grinning, and asked for a towel. She hustled to get him one, as fast as her swollen ankle could go.

He toweled his face and hands, ran it over his hair, then sat at the table, towel still around his neck. Martha had never seen anything so beautiful before. His even white teeth flashed at her through his tan face, as big hands with large, healthy veins grabbed the pitcher and poured two glasses full of cold lemonade. She could only stare.

He wolfed three huge sandwiches, and washed it down with three glasses of lemonade, under her fascinated gaze.

"Aren't you going to eat?"

She'd forgotten! Her little plate of tuna was in front of her, untouched, her fork in hand. She blushed, hoping the powder would cover it up, and took a little bite. Her father never ate like that, did he? Maybe he did. She couldn't remember. She didn't think so. She'd never seen anybody eat like that.

He wiped his hands and mouth on the towel around his neck and sat back, leaning the chair on two legs. "That was great!"

She smiled back at him.

"I'll work the rest of today and tomorrow on the chicken coop, then I'll start on the porch roof." He drummed his fingers on the table. "Yep, I'll paint the coop tomorrow when I'm done. Do you have any beer?"

Martha shook her head.

"Love a cold beer after work. Don't worry, I'll pick some up." He stood, giving a mighty stretch, arms almost touching the ceiling, little hairs poking up above his cutoff jeans. "Well, back to work." He leaned over and gave her a kiss on the cheek. "Thanks for lunch."

Then he was gone, and Martha heard him humming to himself, Skilsaw whining, hammering, and still she sat there, her tuna in front of her, wondering about the new feelings that were creeping up inside of her.

She picked over the garden and cooked the vegetables into a light stew. When she heard Leon throwing his tools into the bed of his truck, she poured more lemonade and sat at the table to wait, but then she heard the truck start, and it drove off in a cloud of dust. Her heart sank to her toes. She turned off the heat under the stew and lay down on the couch. Sadness pressed down on her chest; a tear trickled into her ear. The dimness grew; then she heard a truck turn up her drive.

He's come back. She quickly went to the stove to reheat the stew. It was still pretty warm. He's come back. Oh, he's come back. She went to the bedroom to check her makeup and heard the kitchen door open. No time to fuss with her nose. She walked back to the kitchen, and there he was, putting beer in the refrigerator.

"Hi," he said, looking up, white teeth flashing in his red brown face.

"Hi."

"Dinner smells great. Want a beer?"

"Okay."

He popped open two beers and set them on the table, while she dished up the stew. They ate in silence, Martha concentrating on her meal, trying not to watch Leon eat. Soon he sat back, satisfied. She kept sipping her beer, not really liking it but wanting to do what he did. It was warm by the time Leon had finished off the stew. He stood.

"Let's see what's on television." He clicked it on, and the green newsman warped into view. Leon squatted in front of the set and fiddled with knobs until the newsman's face turned bright red, then settled to a rosy pink. He looked up at her, staring at the set. "Better, huh?"

"Yes." She cleaned the dishes. When she was through, she sat next to him on the sofa, sipping her warm beer, as he drank three more cans. She was feeling very sleepy. Her head bobbed up and down; every time she looked at the television, somebody new was there. Finally, there was just the white crackling, and Leon was sound asleep.

She fetched a blanket, covered him up, and went to bed.

Outside, a rusted truck came slowly up the drive, and with a barely audible curse from the driver as he noted Leon's pickup next to the house, it backed down, squealed onto the highway, and was gone.

CHAPTER 8

Fern's baby was born without a nose. Addie put the squalling child into Fern's weak arms, then tended to the birthing mess. Harry slumped to the kitchen for a shot of whiskey. Fern examined her child, head to toe. The baby looked normal, healthy. Her head was not as pinched nor as elongated as with some newborns she'd seen; in fact, the head was quite large, and square. The fingers, toes, and ears were perfect, but there was no nose.

In the spot where a nose should have been was a thin triangular membrane, thin enough to reveal a network of tiny blue veins under it. The membrane fluttered as the baby cried, and when she took a deep breath and gave her first real scream, it shattered, spraying blood-flecked fluid all over Fern's face. It mixed with salty tears and sweat. She wiped it all from her face, then opened her dress and put the baby to her breast. She sucked hungrily, and Fern watched the jagged edges of membrane flap in and out as the baby nursed.

Addie was busy, cleaning up the afterbirth, seeing to Fern's bleeding, changing sheets, doing everything she could to keep from having to face the mother. She took the soiled linen to the kitchen, handed the bundle to Harry, brewed two strong cups of tea, and without a word, returned to the bedroom, closing the door behind her. She pulled a chair to the bedside and helped Fern up to sip the tea.

In the aftermath of the birthing activity, she noticed how the wind had picked up; she could hear it roaring against the shutters. The room was cool, drying her perspiration.

"I'll fetch Doc as soon as the storm breaks, Fern."

Fern smiled at Addie, her pale face shining with the peace of motherhood.

"She looks strong and healthy enough," Addie said.

"Martha."

"Martha."

Fern watched the baby's face; Addie looked at the floor.

"There's doctors, Fern, that can work miracles on things like that."

"She'll be fine."

"Yes, I know."

"How's Harry?"

"He's getting drunk."

Fern closed her eyes. "Good."

"You sleep now. I'll go talk to Harry. Be real careful not to get any lint in her . . . in Martha's nose, okay?"

"Okay."

Addie went to the door. She took one look back at the mother and child together on the bed. Asleep. It was a beautiful scene, if one did not look too closely. Addie's heart skipped a beat. She closed the door gently behind her.

Addie pulled a glass from the cupboard and sat next to Harry at the kitchen table. She poured herself a healthy shot of whiskey and sipped. He looked at her with red-lined eyes.

"They're sleeping."

"Fern and the monster."

"Not a monster, Harry, your daughter. Martha. Listen, there's doctors . . ."

"Ain't NO doctor going to fix that baby up the way it's supposed to be. It's supposed to be normal, have a nose like everybody else, but it doesn't, does it? God made it that way. *God.* The same God that gives Fern all these . . ."—he groped for a word—"powers, makes her heal all those people, that same God, Addie, made our daughter a monster." The tears broke. "Martha was my grandmother's name. How can I look at that thing and call it Martha?" He took a heaving sob, poured more whiskey into his glass, and drank it down.

"Babies are born with difficulties sometimes, Harry. You have to understand . . ."

"I'll tell you what I understand." Harry glared at her, the anger sharp in his gaze. "I understand that what Fern has been doing is wrong. I told her it was wrong. I knew it was wrong, deep in my gut; I knew she shouldn't be fiddling with what wasn't natural. And this is how we got repaid. God looked down on this little house and saw all that meddlin' going on, and he just said, 'Here!' " Harry smashed his thumb down on the table, like he was squishing a bug. He poured more whiskey. "One sharp rap to the head, and we could tell Doc it was stillborn."

As understanding as she was, Addie was shocked by this. She looked carefully at Harry, upset, wild even, and she knew it was the liquor talking. She was thankful for the storm. She'd have to stay here until it passed enough to go get Doc, and Harry would have to take her there. He would learn. As soon as a doctor put a little nose on that baby girl, and she started to giggle and say da-da, his whole outlook would change. Fathers and daughters, that's the way it was. He'd hold her and coo to her and rock her and love her, and he would never see the little defect the poor child was born with.

But for now, she would get drunk with him, and they would wait until morning, hoping the storm would clear. The silence between them hung like a heavy curtain, Addie already making plans to help Fern get to a doctor who knew these new techniques, Harry making decisions about Martha and Fern and God that would carry him through the rest of his twisted, bitter life.

CHAPTER 9

Priscilla's blue Pinto pulled up to the house just as Leon was showing Martha how to make an omelet for their lunch. Anger flared in her eyes as she noted that the chicken coop was half rebuilt, but no carpenter was in sight. Just Leon's pickup sittin' out here by itself. She slammed the car door and trotted up the porch steps.

She didn't bother to knock, just swung the screen door open. Martha and Leon were standing by the stove, Leon in cutoff jeans and tennis shoes, with no shirt. Martha looking frumpy as usual. What the hell was going on here?

"Pris!" Martha's face lit up with a big warped smile, as she stretched her arms out and went toward her. Priscilla deftly parried her move and stood with feet apart, hands on hips, facing Leon.

"What are you doing here, Leon?"

"Making an omelet."

"Don't be smart. Are you fixing the chicken coop?"

"Yes."

"And sleeping here as well?"

"What?"

"Well, you slept somewhere last night, because you didn't come home."

"How do you know that?"

"Because I spent the night with Ned. At your place. And you didn't show all night."

"Ned? Jesus Christ, Priscilla, isn't he a little young for you?"

"And isn't *she* a little old for you, Leon? You pervert."

"We fell asleep watching television last night."

"Uh-huh. A likely story. So you're here ripping her off for repair work and getting a little on the side, eh? You asshole."

Leon looked at Martha standing there, bewildered, confused, sensing the tension but not understanding. He walked to Priscilla, took her elbow, and escorted her firmly to her car.

"Nothing is going on here, Priscilla. I'm being a friend to an old lady and fixing up her place a little, that's all."

"Is she paying you?"

"Of course she's paying me."

"I wonder if she got other bids for the job."

"C'mon, Priscilla. Don't be stupid."

"You used to fix up around here for free."

"That was . . ."

"That was before you found out she had money. I know all about it. Ned told me about the wad she flashed in Mike's, and you've been here balling her ever since."

Leon slapped her, his heavy hand leaving red finger-marks on her cheek.

Priscilla's eye watered and her face flushed in humiliation and disbelief. She got into the car. "We'll see what your parents have to say about this, Leon." She drove off in a cloud of dust.

Leon stood there, watching the toes of his shoes, until he felt Martha's hands on his arm. They walked slowly into the house together. Leon finished making the omelet. They ate in silence; then he went back to work.

Martha noticed he ate hardly anything. She felt a sadness, an emptiness in the pit of her stomach. Pris, Leon, her two friends. Now neither was her friend. What did she do?

When Leon finished work, he came into the house and took a shower. Martha had a beer waiting for him when he came back to the kitchen, and she sat with him at the kitchen table. He seemed in better spirits.

"I'll paint the coop tomorrow, Martha, then start on the porch roof the day after that. The chickens can move into a nice new house. I'll show it to you in a few minutes."

Martha smiled. A new house for the chickens.

"Leon?"

"Huh?"

"Pris? What . . . happened?"

"Oh, Priscilla. She thinks I'm out here after your money. She thinks we're sleeping together. It's just that *she's* got an eye on your money and is afraid somebody's going to undermine her action, that's all. Don't worry about Priscilla. We're not doing anything wrong. I'll have to talk to Ned, though. That girl is trouble."

All Martha heard was "She thinks we're sleeping together." "Us sleeping together?"

Leon looked at her fondly. "Yes, us. You and me."

Martha stood up to stir the soup. Sleeping together. Her mother and father used to sleep together in the big bed. Sometimes she'd look in there and they'd both be on Daddy's side, with him facing the window, and Mother up close next to his back. It always looked warm and cozy. Sleep together with Leon? Sounded nice.

He drank another beer while she dished up the soup. As they ate, Leon talked on and on about how he was going to repair the porch, and Martha thought only of sleeping with Leon, his smooth warm body next to her in the soft bed. Then she had a new thought. She interrupted Leon's discussion of tar paper and shingles.

"Leon?"

"Huh? What?"

"Why Pris mad?"

"I told you, because she thought we were sleeping together."

"So?"

"So . . . so, I don't know." He waved his spoon around while he looked for an answer. He didn't find one. "Maybe she wants to sleep with you." That was a stupid answer, he thought. "Hell, Martha, I don't know."

Sleep with Pris. Pris didn't seem warm, like Leon.

Leon finished his soup, ate the last piece of bread, popped another beer, and turned on the television while Martha cleaned up.

She joined him on the couch, watched him as he watched the television, tried to laugh when he did. Nice lines in his cheeks and around his eyes appeared when he smiled at the silliness on the screen. He drank beer after beer until his eyelids started to flutter down. Martha turned off the TV with the little box on the coffee table, and listened to the quiet. Not quite quiet. The crunch of tires outside in the driveway. Just someone turning around.

She nudged Leon, and he woke up partially, his eyes not focusing on her face.

"C'mon, Leon. Bedtime." She took his arm and led him to the bedroom, where he undressed and slid beneath the covers. She put on her nightie and got in on her side of the bed, then slid over to cuddle him.

Instantly, Leon was wide awake. What in the hell was she doing? I gotta go home. The thought registered, but her little soft hand was rubbing his arm and it felt so good, so good.

Martha had never felt anything like this before. He was so smooth, so soft, his skin was cool and pleasant. She could stroke him like this for hours. Her hand ran up and down his arm, then down his side, over his hip—he didn't have any clothes on at all—to the little hairs on his thigh. The feel of him made her sleepy. Her hand rested where it was.

Leon rolled over, completely aroused. He knew he was crazy, but suddenly it didn't matter. She was so soft, so nice, so tender. He really cared about her. He pressed against her and ran his fingers lightly over her cheek as he looked at her profile silhouetted in the moonlight shining through the window. Her face was soft; he could see the little tiny white hairs that covered her cheek. He brushed his hand around her neck, down her arm, up over her breast and down to her ample middle. She felt marvelous. He kissed her cheek, then her neck.

Martha was in heaven. She had no idea people did this, but she loved it. She loved him. They would do this every night forever. He began talking to her in a low voice, and feelings began to pulse in her body. He took her hand and put it on a part of his body she'd never seen. She was startled, surprised, but as he told her what to do, she began to enjoy it, she enjoyed it all, she enjoyed him, oh, she loved him.

They stroked and caressed each other for hours, then

drifted off to sleep, only to wake up and begin again. Leon pushed his conscience to the back of his head. He tried to take it slowly, easily, not to frighten her. She was alarmed when his muscles tightened and he jerked and warm wet stuff flowed all over her hand, but he didn't seem to hurt, so she just wiped her hand on the underside of the pillow and didn't tell him about it. The night had a magical quality, a newness, a strange feeling of sleeping but not really sleeping, of someone else in the bed, someone nice, always aware, yet comfortable and peaceful. In the early hours they both slept deeply.

Martha woke up as she always did, when the rooster crowed just before dawn. She felt warm and cozy, drifty, floating. She looked over at Leon, sleeping with one leg hanging over the edge of the bed, the sheet covering his chest to his thighs. His face was relaxed, peaceful, little whiskers growing darkly on his chin and under his nose. His sunblond hair scattered across his forehead.

She snuggled back down under the covers to watch him wake up. She kept to her side of the bed, wanting to touch him, not wanting to wake him. She wanted to watch him wake up all by himself. Feelings of the night before came back to her, memories in vivid detail of the closeness they had shared. She could understand this. She yawned, lazily.

Why would Priscilla be mad? Because Priscilla wants to sleep with Leon, that's why, not because she wants to sleep with me. Why would Priscilla not want me and Leon to be together? What did he say? "It's just that she's got an eye on your money." That's what he said. Priscilla wants money? She can have money if that will make her not mad.

Somehow that didn't feel right. Martha's face screwed

up in concentration. What does money have to do with sleeping together? She thinks I'm paying Leon to sleep with me? That's silly. I'm paying Leon to fix the chicken house. Maybe that's the money Priscilla wants. And Priscilla doesn't want Leon to sleep with me because if he's here every night, he'll work every day, and he'll get all the money for doing other things. Her heart started to pound. She looked at Leon, sleeping, his eyes moving under his lids.

This whole thing is silly, Martha thought. She thought of Mike, and that afternoon in the bar when Leon brought her home. She thought of the other day in the bar with the man with the toothpick, and the one who called her retard. She had answered him: Daddy. Oh, boy, did she really say that? And Mr. McRae in the market. What a nice person. The chickens really liked the food he gave her—what did he call it? Cluck peck. She smiled at the ceiling. Wait a minute. I gave it that name. The smile vanished. In front of all those other people. Shame crept up her face, burning her cheeks. Did I really say that?

Leon moaned and turned onto his stomach. She slid quietly out of bed and went into the kitchen.

It all looked different. There were squished beer cans on the coffee table, leftover soup still on the stove. She thought to scramble some eggs for Leon's breakfast, and went to the refrigerator. Something was really different. Had she ever noticed how dirty it was? There was dust and dirt in the little egg cups, old rotten food in dishes, dirty marks all over the front. She felt a little faint, pulled out a kitchen chair, and sat down heavily. Something was happening to her mind. She looked around the room again. It was shabby, terrible. Something broke inside her chest, some constricting band was suddenly cut loose. She inhaled a great breath and the dizziness faded. Things were so clear.

Automatically, fingers went to her nose, a longtime habit. She went to the mirror in the bathroom and looked at herself. Her twisted nose was still there, the scars were still there, but her lips were even and straight. She picked up a brush and began to brush her hair back from her face; then she stopped and stared. Her eyes. They were a light green-brown, with little flecks of black and gold, and so pretty. They sparkled in the faint light of the dawn that was sliding up over the windowsill. As she watched, the whites reddened, little veins standing out. Tears filled the lower lid and spilled down her cheek. They were beautiful; her eyes were so beautiful.

CHAPTER 10

Fern was exhausted. As soon as the train pulled out of the station, she laid the sleeping baby on the empty seat next to her. Thank God we're finally on our way. She took a last quick check around her, made sure her things were secure, propped a pillow next to Martha so she wouldn't roll out of the seat, checked the white gauze patch that covered most of her face but kept the dust from her nose, and then really relaxed.

She stretched her legs under the seat in front and crossed her ankles. Now she could take a quick nap. The train trip would be most of the day to Chicago; then she had to find whoever was to meet her and go directly to the hospital. Bless Doc Pearson. He arranged everything so carefully.

She missed Harry already. They said their good-byes at breakfast; then Harry went to work and Dave McRae picked her and Martha up and took them to the station. Harry needed to get the fields plowed while the spring weather was just right. As they drove off in the buckboard, Fern waved, trying to catch his attention, but he was concentrating on his work.

He'd been concentrating a lot lately, and none of it was on her or the baby. It had been so difficult. Having a baby was hard work, especially one who needed special care. Fern was constantly changing the gauze patch, swabbing out the cavity, making sure no bath water got inside, in addition to all the other demands a baby made. Harry was no help at all. He barely even looked at the child, which broke Fern's heart.

Whenever Fern took Martha to the bedroom to nurse, she would lay her hand over the child's nose and wait for the healing power to course through her, that familiar feeling, contact with the energies that would help her. But none came. It didn't really surprise her—there was no disease, there was no sickness, and really, growing a new nose was quite out of her realm. The baby was perfectly happy, perfectly normal, and when this doctor in Chicago was finished, she would look normal, too.

This operation would make it all better, she thought. She and Harry and Martha would make a wonderful little family, until there was a little Harry Junior. They would be happy and laugh and play games and love each other.

The wheels rocked an easy rhythm, and soon Fern was asleep.

Chicago was a smelly, noisy place. The train crept through endless miles of tracks that seemed to go nowhere except through an awful stench. She looked out the window and saw nothing but ugliness. Then the tunnel closed about them, and the train stopped. She gathered their things and disembarked with the help of the conductor and walked into the station. She located the clock and went to stand under it, as she had been told. A man waited for her.

"Mrs. Mannes?"

"Yes." Fern took in his young, dark looks and was pleased. He had a nice face.

"I'm Doctor Goldman."

"Oh! Oh, well, I didn't really expect . . ."

"Didn't expect me to meet you here myself? It just happened that my schedule opened up this afternoon, and I thought I could meet you and Martha personally. May I?" He lifted the corner of the baby blanket.

"Of course." Fern shifted her bundle so Dr. Goldman could get a full view of Martha's face.

"Yes, well, can't see too much here. Let's get her over to the hospital where we can really take a look." He picked up Fern's suitcase. "My car's just outside."

In the car, Fern had an opportunity to look at Dr. Goldman. He looked successful. He was dressed well, in what looked to be an expensive pinstripe suit, his car was new, and he carried with him quite an air of authority. He was small-boned, with a large nose, but his eyes were dark brown and friendly, and laugh lines around his mouth showed a face that knew humor.

"How was the trip?"

"Oh, fine. Long."

"I bet. Nervous?"

"Yes."

"Well, don't be. Ralph filled me in on all the particulars of the case, and I don't think we'll have any problems at all."

"Ralph?"

"Doctor Pearson."

"Oh. Do you know him well?"

"We've had a few mutual patients."

"Oh. How long will this take?"

"It will be about three weeks after the surgery before Martha can travel. We've arranged a bed in the hospital for you, so you can stay there."

Three weeks.

The hospital was a bustle of hushed activity. The antiseptic smell, not unpleasant, was pervasive. Dr. Goldman escorted them quickly into an examination room, where he washed his hands while Fern talked baby talk to Martha and settled her down on the table. Then Fern undressed her at the doctor's request.

Very gently, Dr. Goldman removed the gauze patch. As many times as Fern had changed that dressing, it never failed to shock her that under that white square was a gaping hole in her daughter's face. She looked better, she looked even normal with the bandage in place.

Dr. Goldman listened to Martha's heart, checked her mouth, ears, and eyes, weighed her, and wrote down the dimensions of the hole. Martha began to fuss after a while, so after the doctor had applied a fresh gauze patch, Fern dressed her, rewrapped her, then sat down to nurse while they talked. The surgery would be tomorrow morning. No sense in putting it off. It should be easy, routine even. He would take a patch of skin from her hip and fashion a new nose from it, sew it into place with a little metal brace to keep it in shape. It would look a little large to begin with, but her face would grow into it, and in the end, it would be perfect. Easy.

Easy. Fern couldn't imagine such a thing.

A pleasant nurse helped get them settled in their

room. Martha went directly to sleep in the crib; Fern hung her clothes in the little locker-closet by the wash-bowl. It didn't take very long. She wrung her hands, then wiped the sweaty palms on her dress and wandered about the room, it had a nice view of the city, but the city wasn't very nice to look at. Maybe if Harry were here, they could see a few things, but probably not. He didn't know how they were going to pay for it as it was. Fern didn't tell him that the town had taken up a collection. That would be her little secret. It wasn't enough for the whole thing, but it would cover a major portion of the cost, she was sure.

She looked down at the sleeping baby. Absently, she brushed the reddish wisps of hair around on her little head. Such a beautiful child. And in the morning she would be put to sleep and taken into a room where they would cut her side and her face and make a new nose. Fern felt a sympathetic pain in her nose at the thought of it. Time for a walk.

She went out into the corridor of the hospital, noting her room number, 222. Trays of food were being served to patients—the smell stirred up hunger. She'd forgotten all about eating. She went to the nurse's station. A fat nurse stuffed tight into her uniform was writing on charts. Fern cleared her throat, and the nurse looked up.

"Yes?" She had a surprisingly pleasant face, even though her eyebrows were picked almost clean.

"I'm Fern Mannes. I'm staying with my daughter in room Two twenty-two."

"Oh, yes. Have you had dinner yet?"

"No."

"Well, I guess they haven't gotten to your room yet. Why don't you go back in there and wait, and I'm sure a tray will be right up."

"Oh, okay. Um, I was wondering. It's kind of hard just waiting, you know, and I was wondering if there maybe was a patient here that, you know, never got any visitors? Maybe I could visit with them for a while tonight and tomorrow, while my baby's . . . while my baby's in . . ."— she took a deep breath—"surgery."

The nurse stood up. She towered over Fern. "Why, that's a wonderful idea. And as a matter of fact, we have a lovely woman who's been here quite a while. Her son comes now and again, but he's busy with his own family—you know how it is. Mrs. Stimson. Room Two twenty-three, right across the hall from you. She'd be delighted to have some company."

"Oh, thank you. Thank you very much. Are you here . . . ?"

"Three to midnight. My name's Gloria. You give a shout if you or your baby need anything at all, okay?"

"Thank you." Fern felt strange. This was an odd place. She turned to go back into her room, but the thought of that barren place with nothing to do didn't appeal to her. She turned right instead and knocked softly on the door to Mrs. Stimson's room.

"Come."

Fern pushed the door open and poked her head in. "Mrs. Stimson?"

"Yes, what is it?"

"Hi. My name is Fern Mannes. My daughter and I are across the hall. I'm kind of, well, nervous, and thought maybe I could come visit for a while."

"Oh? Well, come on in. Love visitors." The woman was horribly thin; her cheekbones stood out, shadowing hollow eyes and wrinkled lips. She reached a bony hand back to plump up her pillow so she could sit up better, then reached for little tight glasses. She peered out at Fern.

"You're a young one. What's wrong? Female trouble?"

"Oh, no," Fern said as she pulled up a folding wooden chair, "My baby's having surgery in the morning."

"A baby, huh? That's not good. What's the matter with it?"

"Her."

"Hah? What's that?"

"Her. My baby's a her. Martha. She was born without a nose."

"Martha. Always liked that name. No nose, eh? Hah. I'd cut off my own nose if I could live with better veins. That's what I've got. Veins. They've been stripping out the veins in my legs for years now. Damned nuisance."

"That must be very painful."

"Painful! Hah! Can't hardly get around, and a youngster like me ought to be out and about, eh?" She cackled.

Fern felt an irrepressible urge to touch this woman.

"Mrs. Stimson, back home, I . . ."

"Home? Where's that?"

"Morgan."

"Oh, down south. Lived in Chicago all my life, myself. The windy city. Ever been here in the winter, when the wind blows?"

"No, I . . ."

"Terrible. Terrible. People freeze to death just walking down the street. It's so cold their lungs just freeze up on 'em and they fall over. Dead. Just like that."

"Well, anyway, back home, sometimes I can help people who are sick."

"You a doctor?" Mrs. Stimson looked at her with a wary eye.

"Oh, no."

"You some kind of a healer?"

"Well, I'm not exactly sure. Sometimes, though, when I put my hand on people . . ."

"You want money. How the hell does this hospital let people like you in here?"

"No, really. No money. Just let my put my hand on your legs, okay? Just let me try?"

The old woman's face softened. This young thing seemed so sincere. What the hell. Couldn't hurt.

"Sure. Go ahead. No money, mind you."

Fern smiled at her. "No money. Just close your eyes and relax."

"Close my eyes and you'll probably steal me blind." She took off her glasses and closed her eyes.

Fern closed her eyes and shut out all the distractions. Her right hand hovered over the woman's knees. Instantly, she saw the trouble. The passages for the blood were twisted, knotted, dammed up in places, with reservoirs of blood pooling in pockets. They were discolored and sore. Fern raised her left hand to the sky, and a fresh sweet rain poured through her psyche and flushed out the veins. It ran pure and true, straightened out the twisted mess and reamed out the clotting collected on the sides. It emptied and sealed off the reservoirs, dissolved the little tributaries that had been formed out of necessity. When the veins looked fresh and clean, she moved her right hand to the toes, touched them gently, and all the bad blood flowed out of the toes, through her body and out her hand. Then she went back with another cleansing flush and was finished.

She opened her eyes. Mrs. Stimson's face was pink, her breath came in short gasps.

"Mrs. Stimson?"

The old woman opened her eyes, then closed them again. "Just a moment. Let me catch my breath." Slowly, her breathing returned to normal. She signaled for a sip of water. Fern helped her to it. She drank strongly, then fell back onto the pillows.

"Well, I never! That's some power you got, girl. Took my breath clean away."

"Did I hurt you?"

"Well, yes, some of it hurt, but not like it's been hurting. More like a good hurt. Not bad at all." Her eyes opened wide with wonder. "My feet!"

Fern was alarmed. "What? What's the matter with your feet?"

"Nothing's the matter, child, they're warm! My feet haven't been warm in years. Here. Help me get these socks off. I've lived in these cussed socks since I was a teenager."

Mrs. Stimson sat up and pulled off the socks, massaging her feet. They were pink, the gnarled toes flexible. "Oh, my. My, my, my."

"Well, I think my dinner's here now. Is it okay if I come to visit you tomorrow, while my baby's in surgery?"

"Okay? Hell, yes. You come on by here tomorrow, and see if I'm still here. I just might check out of this hellhole tonight!"

Fern walked to the door and opened it. She took a last look back at Mrs. Stimson, who was rubbing her feet, tears streaming down her wrinkled face. She slipped out quietly.

CHAPTER 11

Leslie was in jail. He woke up on that hard, piss-stained mattress with a hangover that would bust the balls off a gorilla. Sonofa*bitch*! He sat up, cradling his head in his hands, but the motion was too much. He lunged for the seatless toilet and just made it, puking and heaving until there was nothing left to come up. He sank to the floor, resting first his cheek, then his forehead against the cool porcelain. What a day. What a pisser.

He crawled back to the mattress, each loud ringing sound reverberating around the inside of his cranium. Why are jails so goddamned loud? He put his hands over his ears and faced the wall. Bright, too. No consideration, no respect.

He drifted off.

He awoke to the clanging of his cell door, and two guards handcuffed him and took him to see the judge. That didn't take long. Drunk and disorderly, one count. Armed robbery, one count. Not guilty, your honor. Bail, five hundred dollars. An attorney will be appointed. Back to the cell.

He was alone and miserable. Armed robbery, what the hell were they talking about? Then the memory of the night before rose through the murky depths of his drugged consciousness. Shootin' his mouth off again in Mike's. God*damn* that Ned. Squealer. Musta been him. Who else was sittin' at their table? Priscilla. Cunt. What's Ned see in her? Somebody else was there, somebody with big tits and a nice tight ass. Oh, Lord, he couldn't even remember her name. Anyway, somebody ratted on him.

He remembered the job, all right. What a score. They were asking for it, in that big fancy house on the hill. What the hell did they expect? Easy, too. Just walked right in. Kitchen door was unlocked. He got no cash, didn't want to go upstairs, but he scored a great hunting knife, lots of silver stuff that he sold for a good price over in Joliet. Good price. Shit. That jack ripped him blind. Always did.

So he shot off his mouth and the cops searched his truck and got the knife and the gun. Sonofabitch. That Ned. Gonna kill that kid.

No, not Ned, he was just a stupid kid. Cops breathe hard on him and he'd spill. No, it was *her* fault. Her and Leon. Him sleeping over there night after night. Two weeks now they been at it. What the hell do they do besides screw?

Leslie rubbed the stubble on his chin. He stood up and yelled through the bars. "Gimme a cigarette! Somebody gimme a cigarette!" The calls that came back reverberated throughout the cold, hard place. "Shut up." "Get your own." "Fuck off." But one cigarette and a matchbook with a lone match in it landed by his feet. He lit up and collapsed back on his bunk. Mouth tastes like shit.

He remembered those nights, just sitting out there, in his truck, radio on low, drinking quarts of Bud, watching the house. He could tell by the lights what they were doing. Dinner, television on, television off, bedroom lights on, lights out. He ought to just go in there and catch them by surprise. In the act. Boy, that would bust Leon up, wouldn't it? He wouldn't, though. He knew he wouldn't. Leon was a lot bigger and stronger, and probably sober, and he'd probably get the crap beat out of him. So he just sat there, fondling his cock, thinking about Leon gettin' into that old retard, drinking beer and smoking cigarettes. It made him crazy.

And Leon was *always* there. He went to the store in the mornings. Other than that, he never left the house. Moved right in, old Leon, moved right in with the old woman.

That's why he hit the house on the hill. He'd counted on that wad of bills from the retard to help fix his truck, but on accounta Leon, it never came through. Leon. That prick. He'll get his, that's a fact.

He dragged on his cigarette until the smoke was hot, then flicked the butt into the corner. He'll get his, and so will she. The familiar fantasy came up to him, the curly-gray-haired retard with her face in his crotch and his gun at her head. Oh, Jesus. He turned over and shoved his hand down the front of his jeans.

CHAPTER 12

Harry met Fern and the baby at the train when they returned from Chicago. They kissed briefly, then loaded the suitcase into the buckboard. People stopped on the street as they passed, waving, calling to her. Hiram McRae and his son Dave came out of the store to welcome them home. Fern smiled lovingly at all of them. Even though her trip to Chicago would forever remain an intense memory of magic and misery, she had missed Morgan during her absence.

She had stayed in Martha's room and prayed the whole day while Martha was in surgery. When she knew the operation had been a success, she walked off nervous energy in the halls of the hospital, meeting people, talking to them, laying on her hands. Many were helped, but Fern learned a disturbing thing while she was there. It was like her fondest fantasy come true, of healing all those within a hospital, but it couldn't be. There were those who would not be healed. She had denied it at first, fought it, wrestled with the bodies and illnesses of some of those people. But it was true, and she began to discern those people as she passed them, barely stopping to speak.

She worked, of course, on Martha, and the healing was rapid. Dr. Goldman insisted they stay the full three weeks, though, not understanding the assistance the baby was being given. He was worried about the grafts taking, and while Fern assured him she was fine, they stayed. And Fern worked with those who would have her.

And now they were home again.

As soon as they had driven through the small town, Harry asked about the baby.

"How did it go?"

"It went well. Doctor Goldman was very nice."

"How much do we owe him?"

"He gave us a special price, Harry. We only owe him fifty dollars. I told him we'd pay him five dollars a month until it was all paid."

"Is she normal?"

"Of course she's normal. You'll see when we get home." Fern was anxious to end this journey. Get settled again.

At home, she put the baby in her crib, then unpacked her suitcase. Harry sat in a kitchen chair, patiently waiting to see what difference his investment had made in his daughter.

Eventually, Fern brought the baby to him. She lifted back the blanket and carefully removed the gauze patch.

"Doctor Goldman said to keep this on for another week or two. At least until there's no chance for infection." She lifted the baby up. Martha looked directly at Harry.

Revulsion welled inside him. Her eye sockets down to her cheeks were still discolored with the bruises of surgery. The stitches had been recently removed, leaving little red dots on either side of a black and red line all the way around the nose. But the nose. The nose itself was as large as Harry's, looking like a beak. It took up most of her face, dwarfing the tiny features of a baby face, and making her appear cross-eyed. It extended from high between her eyes to her lip, and from cheek to cheek. The effect would have been humorous if it weren't so tragic. He wanted to snatch it as he would a Halloween mask and rip it from her face.

Fern saw Harry turn pale. She'd had time to get used to the look of her daughter—this was infinitely preferable to the hole in the face—but then Harry hadn't seen much of that either. She hurried to reassure him.

"They took skin from her hip, Harry, to make this. Look at how perfectly the nostrils are formed. They had to make it big, because it won't grow like the rest of her will. She'll grow into it, and those scars will fade away to nothing, and Harry," she pleaded, "some day she'll look normal."

Harry look at his wife's twisted face. She wanted so much for him to accept this baby as his own, to love her as a father should, but in his shock at seeing what the quack had done to that baby face, he misconstrued her pleading with him, thinking she was trying to convince herself as much as him.

"She ain't never gonna look normal, Fern. She ain't never gonna *be* normal. She's a *horror*!" He shouted this right into the baby's face, and she blinked and began to wail. "Shut it up," he said as he stalked out the door.

Fern's life dissolved in front of her eyes. She unbuttoned her dress and brought the babe to her breast, rocking back and forth in the straight chair. She couldn't think. Fragments of crazy thoughts kept shooting through her mind. Take the baby and leave. Go visit Addie. Go home to her parents. Send the baby away.

Renounce God. Give up healing, give up her life, give up Harry. Kill herself.

The shock of Harry's reaction burned in the back of her throat, but her eyes were dry. She looked down at the little face sucking at her breast, and she loved this child. She loved this little girl with everything in her body and soul, and she loved Harry too.

She raised her eyes to the ceiling and prayed.

Martha grew as a normal child, but by the time she was three years old, it was plain that her nose would never look normal. As she grew, the scars widened, her growing cheeks spreading them apart. The uneven stitching on the left side caused uneven tension, and the nose began to draw to one side, the nostril collapsing in upon itself. And it began to hurt.

After numerous consultations, Doc Pearson finally removed the metal brace from inside the nose, figuring he couldn't do any more harm, and the brace might be the cause of the pain the little girl felt at night. When the metal form was gone, the pain stopped, but the nose began to harden into a twisted shape.

The nose was not the only twisted thing in the Mannes household. Harry had become adamant about the child. She was not to speak to him for any reason whatsoever. She was to be in her room and silent whenever they had visitors. She was never to go to town, nor to school, nor to be anywhere where she might embarrass him. Fern tried, on many occasions, to argue with him, but there was no softness upon which she could make an impression. Harry had indeed retreated.

Fern hoped for another child, a Harry Junior, a boy Harry could wrestle with, but it was not to be. Their marital bed was a cold one, unresponsive, barren. Fern would rub his back, stroke his arms, his chest, but he would turn on his side, or his stomach, and make himself unavailable to her. She was shut out as totally and completely as their child.

One night, she even posed the question. The moon shone through the window of their bedroom. Fern turned on her side to face Harry. He began to turn away from her, when she caught his arm and turned him back. "Harry, let's have another baby."

Harry looked at her closely for a moment. Her bright eyes reflected little sparkles in the captured moonlight. He thought for a brief second about another baby. Thought about Fern's birthing screams, thought about all the blood in the bed. Visions of that first look at his newborn daughter, the constant wishing that she would die. "Don't be silly," he said, and rolled over. It was at that exact moment that Fern realized she needed to resume her healing work in Morgan.

Martha was a joy to her, despite her appearance. It broke her heart to see the child examining herself in front of the mirror all the time, but when Harry was working, they played games, told stories, read, made cookies, and learned the ABCs.

When Martha was five, Fern was able to leave her home alone and go into town. She reestablished communication with the townsfolk, from whom she had, by necessity, retreated these past years. Martha understood everything, her soft little brown curls bouncing up and down as she nodded her head in response to Fern's careful instructions.

Fern felt free as she walked into town for the first time by herself. She stopped and talked with everyone she met, joyous at her freedom. Soon she was going out almost every day.

From her window, Martha would watch her mother go then sit down and read, or play with her dolls, and pretend. But it was boring, and soon she was watching for her mother's return, fantasizing about the things her mother was doing and seeing in town. Then she would see the familiar figure walking slowly down the dusty drive, and her heart would beat faster and she would count her mother's footsteps until she came around the house.

On the hottest day of the year, a black car drove up. Visitors at the Mannes home were rare lately, and the three men who jumped out strode to the door with purpose. Martha hid in her room and listened at the door. They were all excited, talking very fast. There had been a terrible accident—two cars had collided head on just outside town. Both cars were full of drunken teenagers. Please, oh, please, could Fern come help?

Fern grabbed her shawl, spoke quickly and quietly to Martha. "Stay in your room, dear. Mommy's going to go help some people who have been in an accident. I won't be gone long. Please, Martha, don't do anything to irritate your daddy, okay?" Martha nodded.

The four went out the door, and Fern looked toward the field where Harry was working. He didn't see them, and judging by the looks on the faces of the men, there wasn't time to go talk to him. They all got in the car and were off.

Eight kids, two dead by the time she got to the accident scene. She pushed up her sleeves and went to work as quickly as she could. It was agonizing. Delicate and intense. She worked nonstop, with only one brief pause for a cup of coffee. She stopped the bleeding where she could, but the damage to some of the young people was overwhelming.

They had evidently gotten boozed up and were playing chicken on the old road. The crash had broken them like china dolls. She worked on, trying to concentrate amid the din. She stopped the furious flow of blood from first one, then another, then went back to the first and tried to help with the more serious injuries. No sooner had she gotten started than another victim would take a turn for the worse, and she would have to tend to that emergency. She instructed the medics where to place splints and what dangers to watch for, advised them of internal injuries. Without Fern, all eight might have died.

When the sirens faded into the night, carrying their haphazardly patched cargo to the hospital, Fern thought she would faint from the exhaustion. Someone took her to Doc Pearson's house where she had a cup of tea with Doc's wife, and rested up a bit before going home. Then Dave McRae gave her a ride in his dad's new car.

As they pulled up to the front, she sensed that something was wrong. The house was dark and quiet; the front door was open, and so was the barn door. Oh God, she thought. I can't handle something here, too. Exhausted, she told Dave to go on home, and she went inside and turned on a light.

There was no sign of Harry, no note. Surely if there had been an accident, he would have left some kind of message. She called for Martha, but there was no answer. She looked in both bedrooms, under the beds, in the closets. She ran to the barn with a lamp. The animals were agitated, but okay. She soothed them with a brush of her hand as she passed, calling Martha's name, then Harry's. Nothing. She searched the barn for a sign of an accident, a missing animal or tool. Nothing. The barn was clean, as always. She sat on a bale of hay and sighed, worry weakening her to the point of vertigo. She tried to think calmly. Where would they go together, without the truck, without a horse? Why would they leave both doors open? Panic tasted sour in her mouth as her heart started to beat wildly. Something awful had happened between the two of them.

She stood up to go back to the house, and as she swung the lantern around, something smooth shone in the haystack. She approached gently, fearfully, afraid of what she might find, afraid of what she wouldn't find. It was Martha's foot. She dug frantically and found her little girl, staring blankly ahead, naked, eyes wide open but seeing nothing. Dried foam crusted the corners of her mouth; hay stuck to her tongue, hair, and clothes. She was empty.

Fern carried her to the house, quickly, adrenaline chasing the exhaustion away momentarily, and settled her on Harry's side of the bed, dusting off the hay. Then she crawled in with her and tried to cuddle her wooden daughter, who kept staring, wide-eyed, at nothing.

CHAPTER 13

Leon looked at Martha across the table. She needed glasses. She was squinting at a book he had brought her from the library. Her lips moved slowly as her finger followed the line across the page. What is happening here? He sipped his beer and watched her.

"Leon?"

"Hmmm?"

"What's this word?" She pushed the book around to him.

"*Ramification*. It means results, kind of, like one action

has lots of different results in different areas. It has lots of ramifications."

"Oh." She took the book back and continued to read.

He'd been teaching her for two weeks now. In two weeks she was almost out of grammar-school and into high-school reading levels. She knew most of her multiplication tables, too, enough to get by on, anyway. Sometimes the full impact of what was going on in this house drove him to a chair; he had to sit down to think about it. There wasn't anything to think about, really— one day Martha's retarded, the next day she's not. Could their sleeping together have made a difference? Must have been. This line of thinking made Leon nervous; he felt responsible. To be responsible for such a miracle is a wonderful thing, but if he leaves, will she revert to her old ways? He shuddered, feeling trapped, hemmed in, suffocated. He wanted to run, to desert her, to go drive real fast and get drunk with his friends and screw some skinny little whore he'd pick up at Mike's.

And then he'd look at her, or talk to her, or she'd touch him, and his resolve softened and disappeared. He felt committed in a certain way, although she certainly made no demands on him. He'd look at her soft face with those loving eyes and he knew he would be here until she found her way.

Dr. Withins would help. He had stopped by while Martha was reading aloud, a simple book about three kittens. Leon had made sure Martha didn't go into town . . . not yet. He wasn't sure about all this. She saw words on the television and on the boxes and packages from the store and asked him to teach her to read, so he did. Beginning with Dick and Jane. She was very smart, picked it up right away, and when Dr. Withins came in, she was reading. Leon would never forget the look on his face. Thought he'd drop his black bag. But he was cool; he just examined her from head to toe and talked with both of them, a routine examination. Then he took Leon outside to have a quiet word.

"What's happened, Leon?"

"I don't know, Doctor. One day she's retarded, the next day she's not."

"Can't you tell me anything else? Did something happen?"

Leon kicked at some stones in the driveway. He was suddenly ashamed.

"Have you been staying here?"

"Yes."

"Before and after?"

"Yeah."

"And you have no idea what happened?"

"No . . ."

"Come on, Leon. Do you have any idea what importance this has? That woman has been hopelessly retarded for years. Since birth, I believe, although I'll have to check on that. And now all of a sudden, at fifty-four years old, she's regained intelligence, looks like to a normal level. Something happened. Something between you two?"

"Well . . . we slept together one night."

"Had sex?"

"Not exactly, I mean, I didn't . . ."

"No penetration?"

"No."

"But cuddling and caressing and loving?"

"Yes."

"Well, God knows she didn't get any of that with Harry. That might have been all it took." He put his bag in his van. "I'm going to come back and bring some people, Leon, and have Martha take a few tests, okay?"

"Sure. I mean . . . okay."

"Keep her in the house. Let's not let her out at the mercy of the townspeople just yet, okay?"

"Okay." This coincided just fine with Leon's feelings.

"Can you stay on? Want me to talk to your folks?"

"No, that's okay. They know where I am. I've been fixing this place up some, and told them . . ."

"What about your apartment?"

"That's okay. Rent's paid."

"Might want you to stay on here for a couple of months."

Leon kicked some more stones around.

"Okay, Leon? Listen, this is really important to that lady in there."

Leon looked up, intent. "She is a lady, isn't she?"

"She sure is."

"Okay." He smiled. "I'll stay. No problem."

"Good."

They shook hands, and Dr. Withins was on his way. Leon wandered around the yard for a while, then went back inside where Martha waited to continue her reading.

"Leon?"

She broke his reverie. He looked up. She was smiling at him, a soft, gentle smile.

"What's *roguehouse?*"

"Let me see. *Roughhouse*. It means to play hard. Wrestling and that."

"Oh." She returned to her book.

She'd lost weight. She was working in the yard, learning how to plant trees and bushes; her arms had gotten a little tan. She helped paint the trim around the house and handed Leon tools when he fixed the plumbing.

And they talked. She was insatiable for knowledge. They talked about everything Leon knew. She asked questions incessantly—about Morgan, about politics, about how things worked. When they weren't talking, she was reading.

He finished his beer and stood up. "I'm ready for bed."

"You go ahead. I'm just going to finish this chapter."

He slid between the sheets and turned out the light. Hands behind his head, he looked at the ceiling. Dr. Withins was coming by tomorrow and bringing his tests and some other doctors. Leon was a lot more nervous about it than Martha was. He felt responsible, after all. And protective.

His eyes were beginning to close when she came in and slipped into bed, turning on her side away from him. He put his arm around her and drew her close, cupping her breast in his big hand. They nestled together like two spoons and went to sleep.

CHAPTER 14

Harry came home the next morning, offering no explanation of where he'd been all night. Fern smelled the stench of stale whiskey as he passed by her to the bedroom. Martha was tucked into their bed. He gave the child barely a glance as he changed his clothes, then went to the kitchen for a cup of coffee.

"Harry, sit down."

"I gotta get to work."

"The fields can wait. This can't."

He sat, blowing on his steaming coffee, not meeting her eyes.

"Something happened to Martha last night while I was gone. I came home and found the barn door open and the kitchen door open and you gone and Martha under the haystack. This morning she won't talk. Now what happened?"

"I told you she wasn't to go into the barn."

"I have no idea how she got into the barn. That's what I'm trying to tell you. I left to go help at an accident. When I left, she was in her room, and she was fine. Now, she's . . ."

"She's what?"

"I don't know. She won't respond. I'm going to take her to see Doc Pearson this morning."

"Why don't you heal her?"

"Because she's not sick, Harry; it's something else. Like she got scared or something. She's just like a little doll, won't talk, won't walk, just stares."

"Hmmm." Harry picked up his coffee cup and headed for the door.

"Harry, *Harry!*"

"*What?*" His exasperation was evident.

"Where were you last night?"

"Out," he said, and the screen door slammed behind him.

Fern put her face in her hands and cried. Am I that bad a wife? Am I a terrible mother? Why would this happen to my baby while I'm out doing God's work? She shook her fist at the ceiling. "*Why?*"

She cleaned up the breakfast dishes and went back to the bedroom. She sat down next to Martha, whose eyes were closed; she was apparently sleeping. Slowly she moved her right hand along the girl's length, feeling the energy. Her hand stopped at Martha's forehead. Here was a spot that was supposed to feel warmer, alive.

Instead, it was cold, dead. The crown of her head was the same. Nothing.

Fern placed her right hand on the child's forehead, and rested her left palm up in her lap. She waited for the forces to course through her body, to discover the problem with Martha, and to correct it. She waited patiently for a long time. Nothing.

She stood up and walked around the room, loosening her back and legs. Then she sat down again, closer, and put her hand on the top of Martha's head and concentrated, hard. Get inside, get inside the head and find out what's wrong.

The sinking feeling started in the pit of her stomach. It was slightly nauseating, but familiar. She went with it—let's get inside, gently, please, gently, this is my baby, my only baby, what's wrong here, let me find out what's wrong. She felt herself in a dark tunnel, like a mine shaft, with roughhewn walls. Light from an indeterminate source glinted along the chips and ridges in the walls and ceiling. She passed wooden doors, each one locked securely with solid wrought-iron hinges and handles. She pulled and tugged and tried to find locks on each one as she passed, but nothing. They wouldn't budge.

She continued down the corridor, perplexed, looking for an answer; she found herself amazed that the mind held such hallways, such rooms. What on earth was behind the doors?

Then she heard the noise, or felt it more than heard it. A deep, throaty rumbling, so low as to make the floor of the tunnel vibrate. Just ahead she could see a larger door, and the light seemed to come from its translucent surface. Got to get there, got to get that open to release my daughter. She kept on, carefully, the vibration growing as she progressed.

The rumbling increased. She suddenly identified it as a growl, and she stopped, heart pounding, as the nastiness spread toward her. The protective growl increased in volume, a warning to stay away, go away, leave it all alone. She took one more step, and a snarl, an open-mouthed, teeth-bared snarl, made her flesh crawl. The thought of teeth biting into her flesh made her shiver; her next thought—of those teeth rending her daughter's mind—strengthened her. She stepped out again.

Out of the darkness charged a giant animal, yellow eyes bright with fury. Pure-white canine teeth flashed in the light, as foamy saliva flew in all directions. She fell back in surprise, in terror, and the jaws snapped shut on air just a fraction of an inch in front of her.

Fern opened her eyes. She was on her back on the hard wooden floor. Martha was sitting up, staring straight ahead, perspiration standing out on her upper lip. Fern caught her breath and stood up slowly, feeling the bruises already stiffening her back and arms. She sat again on the edge of the bed, and stroked Martha's hand. It was cool and damp. She gathered the stiff child to her and rocked her back and forth until she could feel Martha relax. Fern laid her back down on the bed, and Martha's eyes closed. Soon she was softly snoring the sleep of childhood. In fear and wonderment, Fern sat and watched her sleep.

CHAPTER 15

Leon sat on the couch in a sullen pose, arms and legs crossed, chin resting on his chest. He felt like his space had been invaded, like something personally his was being exposed. He didn't want to share the miracle of

Martha with these three strange men who now sat at her kitchen table, along with Martha and Dr. Withins. He felt the situation being taken out of his hands. Shit, that's what I want, isn't it? Maybe, maybe not.

The tests they were giving her were stupid. "Tell me what this pattern looks like to you, Martha," and "Can you describe your mother for me as you remember her?" and "Did you love your father?" and "What was the first thing you noticed the other day when all of a sudden you felt better?" Silly stuff. When she talked about Leon, his face reddened, and he picked at the couch, trying to ignore them. That stuff is private, dammit!

There were only three things she said that interested Leon. Her dreams about the yellow eyes and snapping teeth he thought were a bit bizarre, but maybe she'd been scared by a dog when she was little or something. Once in a while he had dreams of spiders crawling on him. After all, nightmares are normal. He also thought it was interesting that she remembered her mother as being small, when everybody knew that old Fern was as big as a house. She hardly remembered her father at all.

The only other thing she said that impressed Leon was also what made him so nervous, made him fidget as he sat there listening. She said she loved him, and hoped he would stay with her forever. Christ! He didn't need an old lady to be dependent upon him. He was only twenty-four years old! He liked her all right, but boy, to be with her for . . . oh Christ. He'd have to talk to her about that. A couple of months, Dr. Withins had said. He could do a couple of months.

They sat at the table, drinking coffee and talking to Martha for almost three hours. When they finally left, Leon walked them to the doctor's van. One of the doctors, the tallest one, said he'd like to come back to talk with her some more. There appeared, he said, to be some kind of a psychological block that occurred in her childhood, and was just recently removed, restoring her to normalcy. He wanted to find out as much as he could, because it could be of tremendous benefit to the psychiatric community.

Leon couldn't be less interested. He just nodded, told the doctor to come back anytime, and yawned. It was bedtime.

Then they urged Leon to stay with her, at least until they had a better idea of what happened, both then and now. He agreed, then waved as they drove off.

He went back into the house and went to bed. Martha tidied up the kitchen and joined him. They lay together in silence; then Leon spoke, softly.

"Tell me more about those dreams you have. About the yellow eyes."

"I don't have them since you're here."

"You mean 'I haven't had them since you've been here.' "

"I haven't had them since you've been here."

"Sometimes I dream about spiders."

"Spiders? Spiders are nothing. They're quiet, they just crawl around. These eyes have jaws that snap and growl and come at me."

"Hmmm. Well, I'm glad you don't have them anymore."

"Me too."

"Martha?" He looked at her face, silhouetted in profile against the faint starlight outside. "I can't stay with you forever."

"I know. I just wish."

He turned his gaze back to the black expanse that would have been the ceiling if he could have seen it. "I know. I wish sometimes, too."

"Well, we'll just do till we don't."

He smiled. "Okay. But when I go, you'll be all right?"

She was silent for a long time. Long enough for Leon to count his heartbeats in the quiet, long enough for him to think she had fallen asleep. When she finally spoke, it startled him. "I don't know," she said. "I think so."

He put his arm under her head and snuggled his body close to hers. She felt him fall asleep, one muscle at a time, but she kept blinking to stay awake, suddenly afraid of the nightmare, the one dream that was as real to her as Leon was. Eventually, she drifted off, but her dreams had a presence, a lurking danger pacing the sidelines, ever present, always just out of sight. Even in her sleep, she wondered what it was, where it was, and if it would be with her always.

CHAPTER 16

Doc Pearson took the stethoscope out of his ears and hooked it around his neck. He motioned to Fern that she could dress Martha again, while he sat at his desk and made notes. This was a puzzler. The child had apparently suffered some major trauma, and had totally withdrawn. Only time would tell what kind of permanent damage had been done.

Fern sat in the chair next to the doctor's desk and pulled Martha into her lap. The child looked straight ahead, rarely blinking, seemingly oblivious to the world around her.

"She's perfectly healthy, Fern. I can find nothing wrong with her at all. Her reflexes are fine; her eyes look good. If it was something wrong with her brain, it would have come on slowly; there would have been symptoms.

I think it's been some kind of a shock, a trauma, but what would be so horrible as to induce this type of trance is beyond me. Does she eat?"

"When I feed her."

"With your experience in healing, surely you've seen people in shock before."

"Yes."

"Well, the body goes into a survival stance. Sometimes the feet and hands get cold because all the blood is reserved for the vital organs. What Martha needs is to be kept warm, and she needs lots of loving. I think she'll come out of it just fine, but she'll need lots of care."

"Could a . . . could a dog, or a wolf or something do this to her?"

"I suppose it's possible. Sure, if she'd been attacked. I don't see any marks on her."

"No, I know—it's just that when I tried to look inside, I saw . . ." She saw the skeptical look on Doc's face. "Nothing, it was just an idea."

"Keep her warm and pay a lot of attention to her, Fern. I think she'll be all right. Bring her back next week."

By the next week Martha was walking by herself. The week after that she began feeding herself with her hands. It was two years before she was again toilet trained, and Doc Pearson said the brain damage was permanent. There was only a slight ability to learn. Severely retarded, as a result of a trauma. Fern grew to accept it.

Harry did not. Harry looked into homes for the retarded and spoke daily of taking Martha to one of them, insisting on it, but Fern wouldn't even listen. She wiped the saliva that drooled from the corner of Martha's mouth and talked softly in her ear. They began to fight bitterly over the situation, Harry's voice rising in temper, Fern trying to quiet him down, telling him that it was love and care she needed.

Harry hated the sight of Martha, and razzed and jeered every time she learned something new. When she began to dress herself, she would tend to button her dress wrong or put it on inside out, and Harry would stomp out of the house, shouting that the sight of her made him sick, and something had to be done, because he couldn't live the rest of his life looking at a retard.

Fern understood his fear and shame and anger. Harry was a sensitive man who just couldn't deal with the disappointment of a child who was not right. His faith couldn't handle it. To Harry, God was punishing them all, God hated them, they had somehow gone against his wishes, and had been cast out of his grace. And, of course, it was all Fern's fault.

The first strange experience happened when Martha was thirteen. Fern was in the kitchen, cleaning up after breakfast. Martha was bathed and playing quietly in her room. Then she started screaming. Fern dropped a plate that shattered on the floor and flew to the bedroom. Martha was standing there, blood on her hands, blood on her thighs, screaming, hysterical, out of control. Fern wet a washcloth and slowly wiped the girl clean.

"It's okay, Martha. It's just a little blood, honey. It happens every month. It's normal. It means you're growing up to be a big girl. Let me show you now." And she tried to cope with a new responsibility for the girl. Martha reacted in exactly the same way for six months in a row; then suddenly she began to take care of herself and the monthly hysterics stopped.

Martha grew to be a big girl, strong and healthy. Harry started to give her jobs around the farm, which Fern objected to, but it seemed to put color in her cheeks, and Fern finally gave in and helped Martha understand the tasks at hand. She was good at chopping wood and painting. Fern gave her all the chickens and made her understand the responsibility for feeding them and gathering the eggs.

By the time Martha was twenty, she could cook a stew, fry eggs and bake bread and can peaches. She worked with the chickens and did the wood chopping.

She still retreated to her room when visitors came to call, knowing somehow intuitively that she was not up to it.

Fern was afraid to leave the farm. She'd arrange for someone to stay with Martha whenever she had to go to town or out on a call to help someone. She would never leave her daughter at home alone again. It was a terrible burden, living with her retarded girl and her resentful husband, but Fern accepted it with as much grace as she could. She delighted in visiting with the townsfolk, who carefully skirted the subject of her family except in passing, and talked instead of funny things and unusual occurrences, which helped to lighten Fern's load. The town mourned with this wonderful woman, and they were powerless to help.

At the end of each healing session, when Fern sat with a cup of tea, resting, the people invariably wanted to give her bread or cakes or a roast or a chicken, but Fern would smile at them very gently, pat the generous hand, and say, "The only way you can repay me is to take care of my little girl when we're gone." This brought a tear to more than one eye in Morgan and solemn oaths were made. Each time, Fern felt a little better.

Sam Smith's heart had been going bad on him for some time, and Fern became a regular visitor. She'd sit with Sam, her hand on his chest, and slowly the pains would disappear, his breathing would come easier, and a slow smile would come to his face as the perspiration dried on his forehead. He'd given up all the farm work, hired young school kids to do most of it for him, so he just sat around and gave Addie a hard time as she went about her chores. He never could figure out how he had the bad heart while Addie was so fat. They teased each other mercilessly, but it was all in a loving way. The first time the pains came, Addie was terrified, riding at full gallop to Fern's, and Fern had to bring Martha with them, but they reached the Smiths' in time.

Since then, Fern had come regularly, and sometimes Addie fetched her, but Addie had resigned herself to the idea that Sam wouldn't be around for long. She'd written to her son in North Dakota and had plans to go live there when Sam had gone. She told all this to Fern one day after one of Fern's healings, while Sam slept. She also told Fern that she had already sold the farm, unbeknownst to Sam, but that they could live on it until he died. Half the money she'd sent to North Dakota already, and the other half was to live on, to bury Sam, and for the train ticket to Dakota. Whatever was left over, she said, belonged to Martha.

Fern cried, and so did Addie, the two of them sobbing and holding hands at the kitchen table. It hadn't been an easy life for either of them, but they saw in each other the epitome of the strength of womanhood, and they loved and respected each other as much as any two women ever could.

It was at Sam Smith's funeral that the next strange thing happened to Martha. Fern insisted that Martha accompany her and Harry to the funeral, and Harry complained, but he saw there was no changing her mind, so he agreed. They sat quietly all through the service, Harry noting with intense embarrassment the hundreds of curious glances their way. He reacted by staring them down with a glare.

When the preacher sprinkled dirt on the flowers and the casket, Martha started to squirm around a bit in the chair, then settled back again. Then when the service was over, and they were all standing around not knowing what to say to the widow, Martha looked at her mother, eyes focusing clearly on her face, and said, "I want to talk to Addie." Fern was astounded. She led her daughter through the crowd, and Martha pushed forward urgently, wrapped her arms around Addie in a huge bear hug, then pulled back and said intensely, directly to her, "Sam was good. And now he's better. And you. You . . . you . . ." Her eyes unfocused, her face went slack, the mouth listing again to one side, as she put her head down and walked slowly back to her parents, amid stares and exclamations. Addie just stood there, mouth open, with fresh tears making tracks on her heavily powdered face.

Harry grabbed both his women and hustled them toward the car. Fern looked over her shoulder at Addie, who was staring after them; then she let herself be propelled across the lawn of the cemetery, feeling the anger from Harry, the emptiness from Martha creating a tornado in her own being, swirling dizzyingly, losing sight of reality. She felt faint.

She spent the entire next day working with Martha, trying to break through the barrier again. If she could do it once, she could do it again; maybe there was hope, maybe she could be normal; oh, God; wouldn't that be wonderful?

She worked with her all day, talking to her, trying to teach her. "Come on, honey, relax. Let it come. Don't push it, just let it flow in." Fern's level of frustration reached new heights. She thought of what might have triggered the short moment of awareness. She went over every detail of the funeral she could remember. Addie had sat across the grave from them, her eyes dry, her face hard. Maybe it was the intense emotion. Maybe it was something the preacher had said—how come she couldn't remember much of it? How did Martha know it was Sam in that casket? Whatever it was, she didn't seem to be able to bring it back out of Martha, and she was afraid to go back into her mind, for the fear of the fierce yellow eyes still haunted her.

Fern began to wonder if Martha was indeed blessed with a gift from God. Maybe she just couldn't see it yet. Certainly what she said to Addie was significant. Maybe she was a healer, too. Fern's gift didn't blossom until she was married. Maybe . . .

Fern began to speak slowly and carefully to Martha about God, and about special gifts. She explained to the slack face how it felt when she did her healing work, how she was out of control, and something else took over. She talked to her about how nice it was to have something else come inside her and work through her, and that she must encourage that feeling if it ever came to that. Not to fight it, but to go with it. Fern told her over and over that she was special, God's chosen child, and she must work to break out of her shell and shine her light upon the world. None of it did any good. The girl didn't seem to hear any of it, but she listened quietly.

CHAPTER 17

Leslie was on the prowl. He ground the gears in low and cruised through Morgan slowly, eyes everywhere. Looking for some action. Something. Didn't really matter what, as long as it would take his mind off that fuckin' jail. Jee-sus, what a hole. At a stop sign, he hefted the quart of Bud to his mouth and took several long swallows, eyes searching up and down the cross street. Nothing. Gotta get out of this place, it's nowhere. Yeah, he thought, but go where? He had to make his court date or Ma could lose her bail money. That meant she wouldn't get her diamond back. She hocked it every time. He swigged again, revved the engine, and laid a nice solid strip of rubber across the street. Felt fine. Sounded good. Smelled sweet. The truck jerked as he eased off the gas and continued his cruise, slowly, shifting to second and leaving it there.

He kept going, aimlessly, until he ran out of beer and road about the same time. He pulled off to the side and cut the headlights. He could just turn onto the freeway here and make for Chicago. Or Joliet. Leave this pissant farm town forever. He caught the final drops of beer on his tongue and tossed the bottle into the weeds. He found his pack of Camels on the dashboard and lit one, inhaling deeply. What the fuck.

He jumped out and unzipped his jeans, whizzing into the weeds, looking at the stars, watching the road for traffic. He shook it clean, stuffed it back in his pants and zipped up, doing a little hop on one foot as he adjusted. He kicked the back end of the pickup as he passed. Piece of junk. Back in the driver's seat, he started it up, then made a U-turn. Mike's. Maybe I'll get lucky.

Leslie pulled his rusted-out pickup into a parking spot across the street from Mike's, scraping both tires against the curb. He sat there, finishing his cigarette, watching the door. The whole street was dark, shops closed, quiet, just the streetlights going and the light from Mike's showing through the frosted glass. As the last drag from his cigarette burned his fingers, the door opened, and the street was momentarily flooded with noise—laughter, glasses, squeals, yells, and talk. Two people staggered out, a man and a girl in tight Levi's, arms wrapped around each other as they made their way to one of the cars parked in front. They both got in on the driver's side, giggling and laughing as she slid over—just barely enough for the driver to get in.

"That's what I need," Leslie said softly. "A tight piece of ass." The couple drove off after a lurching start, and Leslie jumped down from the pickup, slamming the door behind him. He tucked in his T-shirt and sauntered across the street.

The humid air hit him like a steam bath. He stood at the door, surveying the place. A typical Friday night. It was packed. Smoke hung in the air like a thundercloud, stinging his eyes. The jukebox was too loud; there were too many people. Not an empty seat, as far as he could see.

He shouldered his way to the bar and got a beer, then turned, one elbow on the bar and one boot hiked up on the rail, looking for somebody he'd want to drink with. He knew most everybody there.

The old folks had the corner booth. They always took that booth; everybody said Mike served them for free so they'd hang around to stop trouble before it started. They did, too. Any loud swearing or rumblings, and the old gents were right there, either cooling it down or escorting the offenders out. Four old men. They played cards.

The rest of the place was filled with young people, with an occasional visitor or old lady boozing it up at the bar. Come closing time, it got real friendly inside Mike's, and most everybody got laid on a Friday night, trading partners around from week to week.

"Hey, Les!" Leslie turned and saw Ned, his face flushed, perspiration running down his cheeks. "They let you out, eh? Let me buy you a beer."

Little asshole. Squealer. "Yeah, okay."

With a beer in each hand, Leslie followed Ned to his table in the back, pleased to see that there were already three girls sitting there, giggling drunkenly. His chances were looking better all the time.

Ned tried to introduce them, but he forgot their names, all except for Priscilla. They'd been shacking up together. Leslie grinned. Priscilla was the target. He'd get that little asshole—he'd take his woman for the night. She was nice, too, a little old, maybe, but a nice bod.

Priscilla grinned up at him, a little drunk, but not too bad. "Hey, Les. Good to see ya. Gee, they didn't keep you long, eh?"

"Nah. They ain't really got nothin' on me."

"Sheee-it," Ned said. "That's not what I heard."

"Yeah?" Les had to keep cool. "Just what did you hear?"

"Be cool, guys. It ain't no big deal. Leslie. Play some Stones on the jukebox."

"Okay. Come pick 'em out."

As they stood up together, the flush in Ned's face got deeper. The other two girls watched silently, with quick glances at each other.

Leslie followed Priscilla's skintight purple jeans as

they wiggled themselves between tables and chairs to the jukebox in the front corner. She stopped, drumming her fingers on the glass as she looked at the selections. Leslie stood just behind her, close enough to feel her body heat, but not close enough to touch. They both felt the heat.

"A-thirteen," she said.

He reached around her, brushing the side of her breast with his forearm as he punched the buttons. He withdrew his arm slowly.

"B-six."

Again his arm snaked around her, his lips so close to the little hairs on the nape of her neck that they moved with each breath. This time the pressure on her breast was more pronounced. She seemed to move into it.

"C-eight."

His arm went wide to the right, so he pushed up against her as he moved closer to reach. He felt her giggle. It turned him on.

"Hey," he whispered into her ear. "Let's split."

She turned around in one fluid motion, so their bodies, and their faces, were almost touching. Not quite.

"What about Ned?"

"What about Ned?"

"I can't just leave him."

"I can."

She giggled again, her cute little nose wrinkling up. She had a twinkle in her eye. A real tease. "C'mon. Get your purse."

"Okay. Be right back." She touched his cheek with her finger, then slid out from between him and the music box. He watched her ass sashay all the way across the room. She picked up her purse and waved a dainty good-night to Ned and the girls, then wiggled her way back to him. Leslie saw Ned stand up, his face red with fury. Priscilla didn't turn back. He put his hand on the small of her back and guided her to the door. He took one quick glance back to Ned, still glaring, and gave him the finger. Then he pushed the door open, into the cooler air, took a deep breath and realized he had a real handful of woman. It felt great.

Her hands were inside his pants before he got the truck in gear. He drove fast, trying to concentrate on his driving, out of town, to the edge of the woods by the Blackman pond. He pulled up short, cut the lights, and pulled on the parking brake. He turned to her, gave her a sloppy kiss, all tongue, gave her crotch a squeeze, and opened the door. "C'mon."

She followed him out, giggling as usual, as he pulled a greasy, stained blanket from the back of his truck. Stumbling, they stepped over the fallen fence and walked through the trees until he found a place littered with beer bottles and other trash. He kicked aside a few things and laid the blanket down, then grabbed Priscilla and lowered her onto the blanket.

Soon they were ripping off each other's tight jeans, and Leslie almost came before he got inside. God, he needed this. He came twice, furiously, humping mindlessly, viciously, and when he finally collapsed on top of her, she rolled him over onto his back and sat up.

"Jesus, Leslie. Give a girl a break." She rubbed her lower back, then fished in her purse for a Kleenex and walked a ways into the woods. Leslie looked into the trees and felt relaxed for the first time.

"Got any beer?" He looked up and saw her standing there, blond bush poking up between her legs. She was shaking out her jeans.

"In the back of the truck. It's warm."

"I don't care."

"Bring me one, too. But leave your jeans here."

She looked at him quizzically, cocking her head. "Leave my jeans?"

"Yeah." He sat up and grabbed them from her, wadding them up and shoving them behind his head.

"Okay." She laughed as she picked her way back to the truck, her wrinkled blouse hanging just short of her solid little buns.

She returned with a quart for each of them. They drank in silence, listening to the sounds of the night. Priscilla sat cross-legged, Leslie absently playing with her curly blond hairs.

"So what, you going to jail?"

"Probably. That little fuck Ned."

"Yeah." She thought for a moment. "You really went into that house while those people were there asleep and ripped them off?"

"Yeah."

"That takes balls. Weren't you scared?"

"Scared? Of what?"

"I don't know. The dark. The people. The guy might have had a shotgun or something."

"Nah. Nothing to be scared of."

"I could never do that."

"Sure you could."

"I'd faint."

"Nah."

They drank again, and the feeling of being in that house returned. He had been scared. It was a terrible/wonderful feeling, that rush of adrenaline. Then he remembered sitting in his truck watching that old retard's house.

"Hey, Priscilla."

"Hmm?"

"Seen Leon lately?"

"Nah. He's been with Martha. Nobody's seen him. Real mysterious. He goes into town now and then, in the mornings, then right back out there. I guess he's moved in."

"With the retard, right?"

"Yeah. She's a nice lady. But Leon's . . . I don't know. It's real weird."

"Go fetch me another beer, okay? Then bring your sassy little bottom right back. I want to talk to it."

She upended her beer and choked down the rest of it, then stood up unsteadily and made again for the truck, stopping to whiz again along the way. When she got back, Leslie was hard as a rock, stroking himself, and she dropped the beers on the blanket and lowered herself onto him.

He sat up, hugging her, rocking back and forth, and whispered in her ear. "Let's go pay them a visit, okay?"

"Who?" Her breath was coming hard.

"Leon."

"Leon. Oh, Leon, okay. Oh, God, Leslie."

They came together, and Leslie pushed her off quickly and stood up. She looked at him, drunkenly, dazed. "C'mon. Get up." He threw her jeans to her.

"What?"

"We're going to go pay a visit to Leon."

She giggled and popped open a beer.

CHAPTER 18

The puzzle of Martha took up most of Fern's waking moments. She tried to fit pieces together—the incident in the barn, the closed doors in the mind, the monster, Sam's funeral—none of it made sense. Trauma, the doctor said. Shock. How could she go in and out like that? How could she have moments where she looked and acted almost normal, when most of the time she was so . . . so . . . unfeeling? And if she could come out once, why not twice, or more often?

Fern bustled around the house, cleaning. She swept and mopped and dusted and hauled the rugs outside to be whacked and aired. She sat down often: the years had accumulated on her, turning her hair almost totally gray; her face was lined and her small frame hung with rolls of fat. As she worked, she thought of her daughter.

There's a purpose to all of this, she thought. There's always a purpose. A purpose for everything, good and bad. At twenty-nine years old, Martha was capable only of basic tasks—cleaning herself, doing some routine chores. She spoke one-syllable words. Most of her vocabulary consisted of grunts and hand gestures, delivered in a moronic fashion. A truce had been set up between Martha and Harry, which kept the house a tolerable place to live. Although it was a constant heartache for Fern, the two ignored each other's existence entirely. She tried to be grateful. It could be worse.

Fern pulled potatoes out of the bin and began peeling them for the stew. Harry was out in the fields, as he was every day during the spring, summer, and fall. He lived for his work; it was all that mattered to him. Occasionally, Fern felt a twinge of guilt that Harry had spent his whole life on this farm, tied down with a retarded daughter rather than having a normal family, traveling a bit, seeing the country, playing baseball with a son—but the guilt was fleeting. Harry had made his own bed.

As far as the farm went, they'd been very successful. There was a solid bank account; Harry had new tools and a good tractor. They'd bought a car, and Fern no longer had to sew clothes for them to wear. They were probably wealthy, Fern thought, but Harry wouldn't part with a dime that wasn't absolutely necessary.

The furniture was in rags, none of the dishes matched, and they could certainly afford to take a little trip or buy some new things, but Harry wouldn't even hear of it. He did bring modern plumbing to the house: toilet, bathtub and shower, a water heater for the kitchen. The rest he considered wasteful excess.

She picked up a fresh potato, one ear cocked toward the bathroom where Martha was bathing. Fern had picked up some fancy bath salts at Dave McRae's store, and Martha sat and soaked among the bubbles until the water got cold.

The peach and apricot trees were heavy with fruit. Next weekend would be reserved for putting them up for the winter. Maybe Martha would help, watch, and understand some of it. Not a difficult process, but exacting if the fruit was to last. How will she ever get on after we're gone? The thought sent chills all through Fern. She tried not to think about it, but the thought slipped in now and again. God takes care of his own, she thought. She'll be just fine. The good people in town will take care of her.

Fern was on her fourth small potato when the gasp came from the bathroom. Fern's heart froze, midbeat, as it always did when an unusual sound came from Martha.

There was no other noise, but a few little splashes, so she kept on peeling.

"Mootheeeer!" A wail shrieked through the house. The knife slipped, skinning Fern's knuckle; she dropped the potato and the knife into the sink, shoved the knuckle into her mouth and ran for the bathroom.

Martha was sitting in the tub, water around her hips. Her hand was covered with soap bubbles, and a look of delighted awe covered her face.

"Mommy. Look!" She held the bubbles up to the light. Fern knelt next to the tub, her eyes on Martha's rapt face.

"Look!" Martha insisted.

Fern looked at the bubbles in the light, colors sliding all around them, swirling reds and blues. In each bubble was a miniature window, with little panes, just like those in the bathroom.

"Beautiful," Martha breathed softly.

Fern looked at her daughter's face. The lips were even, curving in a smile. Her eyes were clear and focused; she looked at the bubbles in amazement, then back to her mother. She held her hand closer to Fern's face. "See?"

"Yes, they are beautiful."

"I never saw that."

"Beauty is all around us, Martha."

Martha sat up straighter, turned in the tub to face her mother. She rinsed off her soapy hand and touched Fern's cheek. Fern again admired Martha's beautiful eyes. Why did she notice them only occasionally? A fingertip traced slowly, carefully, the lines of her cheek, across her cheekbone, one eyebrow.

"Pretty," Martha said.

"You're pretty, too." A tear gathered strength on Fern's lower lid.

Martha watched it with interest, and as she did so,

her mouth began to slacken, one side drooping again, her eyes going vacant, retreating from her face, leaving the horrible nose the dominant feature. The little smile stayed, though.

"Martha?"

Slowly, she slid down into the water, her knees coming up, and she slid back and forth, watching the water lap at the edges of the tub.

"Martha? Talk to me." The moment had come and gone, and Fern knew it, but she wanted it back again. Wanted it so badly she burned inside.

Martha's head turned slowly to her, and it was plain that all semblance of intelligence had escaped. The only thing that remained was the smile, crooked as it was, and Fern wondered if maybe Martha's eyes hadn't finally been opened to beauty.

She kissed the top of her daughter's head and went back to the kitchen to finish dinner, pondering the development—if it was development—that had taken place.

Harry came in as Fern was setting the table, and went directly to the shower. Martha came from her room, dressed, still smiling. It softened her face, gave her a pleasant look. She went around the table polishing the spoons on her dress, straightening the plates, rearranging the glasses, and folding the napkins as she'd seen Fern do on Sundays. Then she went outside.

"Dinner's almost on, Martha. Stay close."

In just a few minutes she was back, clutching flowers she'd ripped up from the garden, dirt and roots hanging below. With that same little smile on her face, she touched the velvety petals of the colored pansies, then held them up for Fern to touch. Fern smelled them first, then touched the petals gently, and the smile on Martha's face deepened.

Oh God, she's getting better, Fern thought. She's responding! She put her arms around her child and hugged her close, tight, rocking her back and forth, afraid to laugh, afraid to cry, this new development seemed so tenuous, so fragile.

She took down a jelly glass from the cupboard and filled it with water. Then she snipped off the roots of the flowers and put them in the glass, slowly, carefully, so Martha could see what she was doing; then she helped Martha arrange them. Martha set them gently in the center of the table, turning them around and around until they suited her.

She watched them, lightly smiling, head tilting this way and that, throughout their silent dinner.

Fern was delighted. Harry pretended not to notice.

CHAPTER 19

Martha heard the truck scrunching the gravel in the drive. The night was cool and quiet, the sound of the truck out of place, menacing in its inappropriateness. She looked over at Leon, sound asleep next to her, the faint shadow of a beard giving his cheeks a hollow appearance in the moonlight. The engine outside died, and she heard the rusted creak of a door opening.

"Leon," she whispered, shaking his shoulder.

He cracked a sleepy eye.

"What?"

"Someone's outside."

"Nah. Why would someone be outside?" His eyes rolled, and his lids closed again.

Gravel crunched underfoot.

"Leon, wake up. Someone's coming."

He opened his eyes again and lay there, patiently. Then he heard it, and his eyes widened as he sat up. They heard a giggle, a low, harsh word, then a soft footfall on the porch steps. Leon swung his legs out of bed and grabbed his jeans, pulling them on quickly. He motioned to her with his hand. "Stay here."

She nodded, her eyes wide with fear, and pulled the covers up to her chin.

Leon looked around the room for a weapon, running his fingers through his hair in frustration. There was nothing.

He walked quietly through the kitchen, looked cautiously out the kitchen window and saw two silhouetted forms on the porch. He waited in the dark, his heart pounding, his breathing loud in his ears.

The doorknob turned slowly and stopped. It was locked. He heard a muffled curse, and digging and scratching. He couldn't decide whether to turn on the porch light or not. Better do it. Maybe they'll just go away. Better than having them inside.

He took two quick steps and turned on the light switch.

Two startled faces looked up at the light, squinting. Leslie recovered quickly. He smiled through the glass.

"Hey, Leon! That you, Leon?"

Leslie and Priscilla. Shit. Both drunk.

"What do you want?"

"Come on, man, let us in. We just came by to say hello." Leslie dug Priscilla in the ribs, starting off a whole new set of giggles. She looked pretty unsteady.

"Get out of here, Leslie. It's the middle of the night."

"Hey, Leon, buddy, just thought you might want to . . ."

"Go home!" Leon snapped off the porch light. He heard Priscilla start to whine.

"C'mon, Leslie. This wasn't such a good idea."

Leslie started to pound on the door. Leon flicked on the light and whipped open the door at the same time. Leslie almost fell on his face. Priscilla stumbled in behind him.

"I'm going to give you ten seconds to state your business and decide to go home."

"Hey, brother. Don't be so hasty. Where's your manners? Come on, how about a beer?"

"Yeah, Leon, how about a beer?" Priscilla thought she was real cute. "Why don't you invite Martha to come join us?"

"I don't need an invitation in my own house," Martha said from the doorway. She was wrapped up in her robe, her hair all astray, hands clutching the robe closed.

Priscilla's eyes opened in amazement. Sobriety settled over her. This can't be Martha!

"Hey, Martha," Priscilla said. "What happened? I mean you look terrific." She belched without even trying to be polite about it.

"What is it you want?"

"Just thought we'd drop by for a little party, right, Priscilla?"

"Uh, right." Priscilla couldn't take her eyes off Martha. "Hey, Martha, remember when we painted the living room, you and me?"

"No."

Priscilla's eyes turned to Leslie. "We better go, Les."

"Not until I get my beer."

"I don't have any beer, Leslie," Leon said.

"*C'mon*, Les. Let's go." Priscilla looked at Martha with something close to fear in her eyes. She grabbed Leslie's

T-shirt and pulled him toward the door. "This is too weird."

Leslie punched Leon lightly on the arm. "Take it easy, eh, Leon? Maybe we'll get together for that beer soon." He followed Priscilla out the door. "I'll come back."

"There'll be a shotgun waitin' next time, Leslie."

Pure evil rippled across Leslie's face. His arms hung limply at his sides, as if the beer were finally catching up with his body, but his face sneered. He whispered menacingly. "You fuckin' pervert."

Leon clenched his fists and stood his ground, watching as Priscilla grabbed Leslie's T-shirt again and pulled him out to the truck. Leslie stumbled backward, then jerked out of her grasp, eyes clamped tight on Leon's.

They both got in on the driver's side, and Leslie started the engine. It coughed. He wanted it to roar. When it caught, he tried to spin around, spitting gravel fifty feet behind him. Instead, the truck died, and the headlights dimmed again and again as he ground the starter. He cursed it to life, and the truck with its two drunken passengers lurched out of the drive as Martha and Leon watched them go.

"Take me home, Leslie," Priscilla said. "I don't feel too good." She leaned out the car window and puked.

"Sonofabitch! All over my truck, you cunt. I'll get your ass, Leon, and that weird retard, too. Son of a *bitch*!" He pounded on the steering wheel.

Leon turned out the light and locked the door. He went to Martha, standing in the doorway, staring straight ahead. She was trembling, and perspiration stood out in little drops on her forehead.

"Martha? You okay?"

"I don't know. I feel ... for a moment there, I felt

... while you were in here and I was in the bedroom, I almost ..."

"Shhhh." He put his arms around her and held her close for a moment, then guided her gently back to bed. He got in next to her and held her, a very young man and his very strange lover. He did love her, in a way.

"I felt out of control, Leon."

"Fear can do that. I was afraid, too."

"Out of control?"

"Not exactly, but men are supposed to be braver than women."

"This wasn't brave, or scared. This was ... was ..." she shuddered. "Something else, like taking hold. Inside."

"They're gone now. And they won't be back."

She leaned up on an elbow and looked at his eyes, shining in the faint light.

"Promise?"

"Promise."

She lay back down and traced the lines of his cheek with her finger, trying hard to forget the terrible, terrible feeling.

CHAPTER 20

Harry limped in from the fields about ten o'clock one morning, his left arm hanging useless at his side. Fern took a look at his pale face and knew he was dying. Her healing powers had become so attuned to life that she could discern the least imbalance. Harry had been not well for about a week, and today he would die.

Oh God, she thought, where have our lives gone? She knew it was coming. They were not young anymore; Harry still drove himself too hard, he was never happy.

God had not gifted Harry with laughter. Life was a serious business to him, not something to be joyous about.

She looked at his gray, worn face and flashes of their relationship flitted through her mind. The good times. The times when they had made love, when they were courting, the oftentimes humorous things he would say by mistake, his embarrassment at her laughter. She saw him as he used to be—young, virile, handsome, and muscled. Where did all the years go?

Now he was old and gray, skin matching closely the yellowed color of his hair. His face was wrinkled and marked with brown spots. We should have retired years ago, she thought.

She dried her hands on a kitchen towel and put her arm around him, helping him to the bedroom, where she undressed him and put him into bed. She sat on the edge, smoothing the hair away from his pale forehead. He'd had a stroke. His body was worn out. If she were to heal him now, there'd be another one tomorrow.

"There's nothing I can do, Harry."

His gaze wandered over the room, avoiding her face.

"We've had a good life together, you know."

The breath caught in his throat. He closed his eyes, resting for a moment. Then he looked up at her, moistness collecting in the tanned wrinkles around his eyes. "How can you say that, Fern?" The words were slurred, his tongue thick.

"Because I've spent my life with the two people I love. That's all."

"It's been hard. I've been . . ."

"It's not been easy. But then . . . that's how it is, sometimes."

"You've been a good wife." He reached for her hand and pressed it to him.

"Don't be afraid, Harry."

She reached down and kissed him slowly, tenderly, on the cheek. He closed his eyes and died.

She pulled the covers up to his chin, smoothing the quilt that had been his parents', that had been on this bed when he was born. The empty ache inside her burned like a fire, from the pit of her stomach up through her throat. The tears were lumped behind her eyes, but they wouldn't come. She wandered around the room for a moment, hanging up his work clothes, touching his things, then she went back to the kitchen to finish the breakfast dishes.

Martha, sensing a difference in the atmosphere of the house, came out of her room and sat quietly at the kitchen table, waiting. Fern poured a cup of coffee and sat down next to her, taking her hand. Martha's hand was not young, and hers looked like a claw on top of it. She sipped.

"Your father died."

Martha nodded.

"I loved him very much."

Martha nodded again. Suddenly the flow of tears burst forth and Fern sobbed, her head on her arms, shaking uncontrollably. She cried for all the lost good times of their lives, for the retirement she had hoped to have. She cried for the shattered dreams they had once shared, of selling the farm and moving away, of having a houseful of children, of being a close family, full of joy and laughter and fun. And she cried for Harry, a worn-out man, unhappy with himself, bitter and mean in his way, so afraid, so afraid.

The tears ebbed; she caught her breath, blew her nose on the tissue Martha brought. She looked at their daughter and thought to cry again, but she'd chosen her path in life, with Harry and Martha, and there was no room for self-pity here. Not now. There was too much to do.

She sniffed, regaining control, smiling weakly. "I have to call Mr. Simmons."

She dialed the black phone and counted the rings. Mr. Simmons answered.

"Fern Mannes, Mr. Simmons. Harry has died."

She listened.

"That will be fine. Thank you." She hung up and turned around. Martha was gone.

Fern walked into the bedroom, and found Martha sitting on the edge of the bed, just as she had moments ago. She was touching his face, his eyes, his nose, his lips. Fern just watched, leaning against the doorway. Is this the first time she's ever touched him? This little girl who now had gray in her hair and wrinkles on her face? The tears pushed again, but she held them back.

"He's quiet," Martha said.

"Yes."

Fern rode into town with Mr. Simmons and his aide, with Harry in the back and a metal box of papers on her lap. The black car paused at the curb outside the bank, and Fern got out, said a few words to Mr. Simmons. Then he drove off and she went inside. An hour and a half later, she came out and walked across the street to Dave McRae's store, then to the post office, and the dress shop, and each store in turn. The more places she went, the faster she began to walk, the more intense was her mission. As she walked out of the last shop in Morgan, she was exhausted. She stood on the curb, perspiring, breathing heavily with the exertion of the emotional work she'd been doing.

She stood there for a moment, leaning against a

street-lamp, looking down the street with its parking meters and cars, with the neon signs and fancy manne-quins in the windows, and remembered how it was that one hot and dusty day forty-nine years ago when she walked through this street as Harry's bride. She could feel the heat, smell the dust as it caked inside her clothes, in her throat. She was small then, thin, and carried two heavy black bags, and she was so in love with her man. What had happened to that love? Nothing, really, love was love.

Fern turned down the street and began the trek home. Her feet ached. A car pulled up next to her and Dave McRae looked out at her. "Give you a lift, Fern?"

"No thanks, Dave. I need to walk a little more."

"Pretty hot day."

"I'm all right."

"Okay. Take it easy." He drove off, leaving Fern standing there, sweltering in the heat, drowning in her memories.

She began walking again, mentally making a list of all the things she needed to teach Martha. With Harry gone, the reaper wouldn't be wasting any time coming for her. Martha would be in good hands in Morgan, as long as she was meticulous as she laid all the groundwork.

Just as she turned down the drive, a pain erupted in her chest. It reached out her arm to the fingers, dragging with it a bale of barbed wire. She didn't know whether to bring her hand to her chest or fling it away; it was just a foreign appendage, and it hurt like bloody hell. It was a terrible thing, the pain, and it brought not so much panic and fear as sorrow and a more urgent prayer that her time not be up yet. She clutched at her breast, then sat down heavily in the middle of the road, rubbing her hand, her arm, tears flowing silently, freely down her face. Not yet, please God, not yet. I have to take care of Martha first.

She lay down gently in the road. The pain subsided slowly. When it was gone, she got up and walked carefully to the house.

CHAPTER 21

Leon finished loading the truck with trash for the dump, then went into the kitchen to wash his hands. "I'm leaving now, Martha. I'll be back in a couple of hours."

Her voice came from close behind, startling him. "I'm going with you."

He looked her up and down. She looked terrific. Her gray hair was brushed up and held with a pin in the back. She had some makeup on, powder, lipstick, and what looked to be a new dress, belted in at the waist. "Are you sure?"

"Yes."

They got settled in the truck, and Leon drove slowly toward town. "Where do you want to go?"

"The bank. The store."

"Okay." Uneasiness filled him. This was The New Martha's first venture to town. No telling what the townsfolk would say. "Want me to come with you?"

She looked directly at him. "You're going to the dump."

"I can always go to the dump."

"No. I think I'll go alone."

"Okay."

He dropped her off in front of the bank. "I'll pick you up right here." He smiled.

"Okay." She took a quick look in the side mirror,

adjusted her dress, and walked away. Leon wanted to go with her, but he suppressed his protective instincts and instead gunned his engine and headed for the dump, determined to be back as soon as possible.

The bank was cool and expansive, with a slight sickening odor she remembered. She went to the first person she saw, a redhead at the teller window.

"I want to talk about my money." The girl's eyes widened in recognition and disbelief. She came forward to look closely.

"Martha?"

"Yes." Martha smiled.

The girl cleared her throat, recovering from her surprise, "Just a moment. I'll bring over Mr. Hillis."

Martha folded her hands in front of her and waited quietly.

Soon a little man in a suit came hurrying over, talking quickly and quietly to the redhead. As he approached, an uneasy smile spread across his face. He held out his hand.

"Miss Mannes. How good to see you."

Martha looked at his hand and held out her left one. The man squeezed it gently, then led her back to his desk, in the corner of the big room. "Please. Have a seat. Some coffee?"

"No. I want to talk about my money."

"Fine. What can I tell you?"

She looked blank. "Everything."

His smile faded. "Everything. One moment." He pushed a button on a little box on his desk and spoke into it. "Julia, please bring in the Martha Mannes file." He sat back and studied Martha. "You look well."

"Thank you. I feel good."

In a moment, a tall, thin girl placed a thick folder

on the desk. Mr. Hillis put on a pair of half glasses and began to sift through papers.

"I assume you know nothing of your financial status?"

"Nothing."

"Okay. Let's start from the beginning. There is a trust in your name, a gift from Mrs. Addie Smith. The original amount was for just over twenty-five hundred dollars, but it's grown now to . . . let's see . . . almost nine thousand." He took off his glasses and smiled at her. "We invest our clients' money wisely." She just looked at him, trying to understand. "Ahem. Then there was your parents' estate. They left everything to you, of course, and your mother, uh, Fern Mannes, left the bank here as trustee." He took down his glasses again, and looked at her. "That means, Miss Mannes, that we would take care of you, give you the money that you need, and when you . . . uh, died, the rest was to be given to the various charitable organizations that your mother worked with while she was alive."

"How much?"

"All together?"

"Yes."

"Well, just a moment." He fingered a calculator, riffling pages as he went. "Not including the farm, let's see. Not including the farm, I see a net worth here of one hundred thirty seven thousand dollars."

"Would you write that number down for me, please?"

"Certainly." He tore off the calculator tape, circled the last number and handed it to her.

"And to get money, I just come in and ask for it?"

"Yes. But please, don't spend it all."

She smiled at him for the first time. This was very tiring. "I just want some new furniture."

206

He grinned, broadly. "You just tell the store to send the bill to me. Within reason." He handed her his card.

"Ran-dolp Hiles."

"Randolph Hillis."

"Thank you."

"My pleasure." He walked her to the door, but before he opened it, he leaned closer, and whispered conspiratorially. "Miss Mannes . . ."

"Yes?" She smiled.

"Um, we've seen you in here a lot these past years, since, uh, since your parents died. And, I must say, I've never seen . . . um . . . well, you're looking very good."

"You mean—what happened?"

"Um, well, yes, I guess that's my question." He began to wring his hands.

"I don't know, Mr. Hillis. Good-bye." She walked out the door into the warm air, and looked up and down the street.

Hillis turned to face the wide interior; every eye was on him, questioning. He shrugged his shoulders and went back to his desk. He canceled his appointments and went to church.

Martha walked across the street and entered the McRae store. Dave was putting a new tape in the cash register. He looked clean and fresh in his white shirt, his bald head nicely tanned, the gray fringe around his head combed neatly down. He looked up briefly as she entered, then went back to his work.

"Hello, Martha," he said. "Long time no see."

"Yes," she said. "It's been a while."

Slowly his head came up to look at her smiling face. Jesus Christ! His face reddened; he cleared his throat. Such shocks were not good for the heart, he thought. He smiled. "Bring me any eggs?"

"No. I want to talk to you about my mother."

Dave came around the counter and took both her hands in his own. "You look pretty as a picture, Martha. I'd never have believed you'd look this nice. What's happened in your life?" God, her eyes are absolutely beautiful, he thought. Like sparkling snowflakes inside.

"I don't know. Something."

"Something indeed. I'd be delighted to talk about your mother. A dear, dear lady." He showed her his forearm, where a thin white scar ran the length from the wrist to the elbow. "She did this for me."

"She cut you?" Martha was horrified.

"No, no, dear, no. I cut myself helping your father when I was just a lad. He half carried me into the house. I was bleeding terribly. And your mother laid her hands on the cut and healed it."

"She healed it?"

"Yep. Worked miracles, that woman. A natural healer."

"Did she ... ? Did ... ?" Martha groped for the question.

"Did she heal a lot of people? Most everybody in town was helped by your momma at some time or another. A wonderful woman, she was, yes indeed." His eyes looked beyond her, far into the past.

"And father?"

"Your father was a farmer, Martha. No more, no less. Your momma loved him with all her heart, as she did you. She didn't have an easy life. Harry was set against her healing, but she did it anyway. And brought you up at the same time. And look at you now! Glory be, I wish Fern were here to see you now, looking so sharp, standing in my store."

"Mother was a healer." A faint memory tickled at

the back of her head. *"You're a very special girl, Martha. Someday everyone will find out just how special you are."*

"Yes, she was."

"Thank you. I have to go now."

"You're welcome, Martha. Come back anytime." He opened the door for her, and touched her shoulder on the way out.

When she'd gone, he sat in the folding chair he kept next to his counter and delved into memories of his youth, with a sweet-sad smile on his face.

Leon was waiting in his truck, parked in front of the bank. He sat up straight when he saw her come out of the McRae store, then reached across and opened the door for her. She got in and smiled at him.

"Leon," she said as she opened her purse and took out the tape Mr. Hillis had given her, "is this a lot of money?"

Leon looked at the circled figure and whistled. "Yes. A *lot* of money."

"Enough for new furniture?"

"Yes."

"And a new truck for you?"

"Oh, Martha, come on."

"I'm serious. Is it?"

"Yes."

"Let's go."

He kissed her on the cheek and put the truck in gear. Mother was a healer, she thought.

CHAPTER 22

Fern sat at the kitchen table, note pad and pen in front of her. The pressure inside her head was tremendous. Martha sat next to her, watching the tortured look on her mother's face. Fern tried to think of everything she needed to teach Martha, everything she needed to know in order to get along on her own. It was a heartbreaking task.

With pictures she wrote out the recipe for a stew, and for a vegetable soup. She made grocery lists, pinning together labels from all the canned goods and things Martha liked to eat. She showed Martha how to wash clothes, rinse them well, and hang them on the line. It was hard—Martha's attention span was so short. She had to talk quickly, with lots of action. They went to the yard to look at the vegetables and the chickens.

"Most important, Martha. Martha, concentrate. Most important, feed the chickens. The chickens gotta eat. The chickens gotta eat. If you have chickens, you have fresh meat and eggs, okay?"

At this, Martha brightened. She loved the chickens. "Okay!" she said.

Fern laughed. "*Okay!*"

"*Okay!*" Martha imitated her. They hugged each other. She'll be all right, Fern thought. A hot tear started to form again in Fern's eye. I've had enough crying, she thought. Martha pointed at it, questioning.

"Dust," Fern said, swiping it away.

When Fern announced they were going to town, Martha's eyes got shiny and excited. She picked out her favorite dress and slipped it on, then watched her mother get ready, watched her brush her long gray hair, then twist it up in a bun. She powdered her nose and put on red lipstick. This routine fascinated Martha, and she was content to watch, anticipation of the trip to town forgotten as she shared this time with her mother.

They walked quietly down the road, nervous energy

flowing through Martha, a dreaded heaviness in Fern.

First stop was the bank. Mr. Hillis saw them coming through the doorway and came right up to meet them. He introduced Martha to each of the tellers, and together he and Fern explained that this is where she should come for money to go to the store. "Just come in and ask for twenty dollars," Fern told her several times. Martha seemed to understand. Mr. Hillis had suggested that she just open an account with McRae's, to be paid by the bank, but Fern wisely suggested that Martha needed more contact with people—she would be so alone at the farm. Mr. Hillis agreed, and so it was settled. A wise old woman, Mr. Hillis thought.

Martha cheerfully smiled her crooked way at all the pretty girls in the windows. They all smiled and waved to her until she was embarrassed and turned toward the corner window to look at her reflection. Fern thanked Mr. Hillis, waved to the girls, and took her out.

They looked both ways before crossing the street and going into Dave McRae's store. Dave had inherited the store when Hiram retired ten years ago. He was a very pleasant man, eager to help. When Fern told him her mission, he could see the wisdom in her actions, but was saddened to think that this wonderful woman would eventually be taken from their lives. And it was with sadness in his face that he greeted them both on this important day.

"Mr. McRae will be your best friend, Martha. Your friend." Martha smiled up at him shyly. "Whatever you need, you come here, see Mr. McRae, okay?" Martha wandered off, looking at all the bright packages and bottles and cans and jars, while her mother and the nice man with no hair talked. Soon she was called back.

"Concentrate now, Martha. You get money at the

bank, and you bring it here, okay? Mr. McRae will give you flour and milk, and the other things you need, okay?"

"*Okay!*"

Everyone chuckled, and Dave put his hand on Martha's head. "She'll be fine, Fern. We'll all see to it." He reached in a jar and brought out a candy stick which Martha promptly stuck in her mouth, sucking loudly.

"Thanks, Dave." With her daughter in tow, Fern continued through the other shops in town. The reception was much the same. Everyone seemed cooperative, but how could she be sure? Trust, she told herself. Trust.

When they finally got back home, as tired as Fern was, she continued to make telephone calls. She called Mrs. Martin, the woman who worked with the 4-H. Of course, Mrs. Martin said, she'd be delighted to keep up Martha's garden as a project. She called Penelope Wiggins, whose daughter had gone to beauty school. Of course, said Mrs. Wiggins. Priscilla would be delighted to come and take care of Martha's hair. Priscilla doesn't remember, of course, the fever she had that called you out of bed in the middle of the night, but I do. I'll remind her. She'll be glad to do it. Thank you very much, said Fern.

Fern's mortality was closing in on her. Never had her own death seemed more real. It was coming closer; she could feel it. She knew what health looked like and sickness, and death, and she felt the black cloak descending on her increasingly fragile bones, and the thought was almost comforting.

After she'd made all the calls she could think of, she remembered the animals in the barn. They hadn't been tended to since yesterday morning, when Harry had done it. Was that only yesterday? Oh dear, his funeral is tomorrow. There's so much to do. Must find someone to tend the animals, or to take them away. Martha was afraid of the barn.

Fern rested for a moment, then went to the barn. She shoveled and hosed, then spread new hay. She checked the feed for the cows and horses, and when all was done, she got the stool and sat down to milk.

The easy rhythm of the milk in the pail began to ease Fern's mind. There was just so much to do, so much, so much. Find someone to take the animals . . . and what else? Everything else. How could she leave her daughter? Why hadn't she thought of this before? Why hadn't she sent her away as Harry had begged her to do so long ago, then have normal children who would be taking care of her in her old age, instead of this? Oh, please, God, take care of my . . .

The pain grabbed her chest again, knocking her back from the stool. For a moment she thought she'd been kicked. But it kept up, her breath, she couldn't get her breath, couldn't move her arm, her hand, my God, it was on fire. Her right hand clutched and tore at her clothes, get loose, get loose! Give me air, breath, oh, God, not yet, please, I have one more thing to do, just one more thing, just one more try, please, oh, God, please.

CHAPTER 23

Leslie saw the Bronco come down the street just as he was ready to jump into his own rust bucket. He stopped instead and watched it approach. It was beautiful. I'd give my left nut for something like that, he thought.

The new truck had giant tires, lifting it high off the ground. It was painted in two colors, a bright green-blue and cream. It had lots of chrome—even the lug nuts on the wheels were shiny and silver. It had driving lights mounted below the grill, with their little yellow slip-covers still on. Looked brand-new. What a beauty. Admiration turned to envy, then quickly to disgust. Some rich motherfucker who won't take care of it. I'd take care of that baby if it was mine.

The Bronco cruised slowly through town, then pulled into a parking space next to the bank. Leon hopped out.

Leon! That sonofabitch! Leslie's fists clamped hard, and he slammed shut the door to his truck, feeling the whole rusted-body shimmy with the impact. Leon walked around the front of the new truck and toward the bank. Leslie ran a few steps to catch up, then slowed to a walk before he called out.

"Hey, Leon."

Leon turned, smiling, then scowled as he saw Leslie's toothless grin.

"Hey, Leslie," he said softly.

"Where'd you get the buggy?"

"Oh, nice, isn't it?"

"It's okay. Say, where'd you get the bread for it?"

This guy's got more nerve, Leon thought. "It's Martha's."

Leslie hooted. "Martha's? Martha don't drive. You mean she bought it for her little gigolo, eh, Leon? You pervert."

Leon walked toward the bank, turning his back on Leslie.

"Think I might take a tire iron to this pretty paint job tonight, Leon. Yep. That big ole windshield ought to just crack into a million little spiderwebs."

Leon took three large steps backward and grabbed Leslie by the arm. He was surprised how small the other man was; they'd never really gotten this close. His hand went all the way around Leslie's skinny wrist.

"You touch that truck and I'll bust your friggin' head, Leslie."

"Let me go."

"Leave us alone, you hear?"

"I hear, I hear, now let me go."

Leon increased the pressure as he stared into Leslie's face. "I mean it!" He threw the arm down. Leslie caught it with his other hand and began rubbing the red skin.

"Cheez," Leslie said as he turned away. Leon watched him. As he passed the rear end, he reached out with his boot and gave the tire a hard kick, but the rubber bounced his foot right back.

"I'm warning you, Leslie. Stay clear."

Leslie got into his truck and roared off, sticking his finger up at Leon as he passed.

The bank could wait. Leon got back into the truck and started it up. It smelled so good, brand-new. Like sitting on top of the world and driving, it was so high. It felt real strange. It was even stranger, knowing that everybody knew that Martha had bought it for him. But that's okay. She's a good lady and I'm proud of her.

He grinned. Hey, I am, he thought. He tried it out loud. "I'm proud of her," he said to the rearview mirror. It sounded good. Suddenly, he wanted to see her more than anything, so he put the truck in gear and drove down the road.

Leslie drove to the edge of town, fuming. That prick! He gets all the cash; I get to go to court. Tomorrow, gotta go to court tofuckinmorrow. Gotta get drunk tonight. And laid. That prick. Suddenly, he slammed on his brakes and brought his truck around in a full turn and headed back for town. He pulled up in front of Shirley's Hair Salon and got out. He fished in his pants pocket and pulled out a crumpled wad of ones and fives. He looked it over, then pushed open the door of the flower shop next to where Priscilla worked.

"May I help you?" It was old Mrs. Watson. Leslie had her for homeroom teacher when he was a sophomore.

"Can I buy a flower or something for about a dollar?"

"Our roses are ninety-five cents."

"Yeah. A rose."

"Would you like to choose one? They're right here."

"Nah. Any one."

"Here's a lovely red one. Fresh." She held up the flower. "Why it's you, Leslie. How are you?"

He looked at the flower, at her smile, then at the floor. "I'm okay. I'll take that one."

"All right." Mrs. Watson took forever putting a white bow on the stem, then wrapping it in thin green paper. She stapled the end and handed it to him. He put his crumpled bill on the counter.

"Nice to see you again, Leslie."

"Uh, yeah, nice to see you too." He walked outside, then in through the beauty-shop door, feeling very out of place around all the smells and girlie things.

Shirley stuck her head around the corner. "May I help you?"

"Priscilla here?"

"She's with a client right now, if you'd care to wait."

Leslie looked around uncomfortably. He didn't want to wait. "Can you just tell me when she'll be through?"

"I'll be right there, Shirley," Priscilla's voice came up from the back. She walked out, holding up her hands, covered in plastic gloves and dripping brown goo.

"Hi," she said.

He held out the flower.

"For me? How nice." They both looked at her gooey hands, and she lifted up an elbow. He tucked it under her arm. She tried to smell it but was in danger of touching the brown dye to her hair.

"What time you get off?"

"Three." They both looked at the clock. "I have to finish the head I'm on, then I have another appointment for a cut."

"C'mon," he whispered. "Get someone else to do it."

She giggled. "Leslie, I can't do that."

He leaned in close to her, whispered in her ear. "I just gotta have you. Now."

"Come back at three," she giggled over her shoulder, with a cute backward glance.

"Okay. Meet me at Mike's."

"Okay." She blew him a kiss.

An hour. Shit. He walked out of the tinkling door and down the street. An hour at Mike's.

Leslie got the idea when he was taking a whiz about ten o'clock. It was probably the greatest idea of his life. Mike's was packed as usual, Priscilla was getting giggly and cute as hell, Ned was fuming over in the corner by the old dudes, and Leslie was looking better each time he looked in the men's-room mirror.

He combed his hair back and admired himself. Yep. One hell of a good idea. We'll go pay Leon and Martha another little visit. Only this time it won't be like last time. This time I'll do the talkin'. He grinned in the mirror, then did a little two-step.

Back at the table he gave his beer away and ordered a cup of coffee from the bar. Priscilla looked bleary-eyed at the coffee. "Coffee?"

"Yeah." He leaned close to her. "Can't get too drunk tonight."

She smiled up at him, brows together in mock seriousness. "Oooh, I know what you mean." She moved her hand up on his leg.

"Not that, Priscilla. I'm going to pull a job tonight. If you want to come, you better sober up."

"A job? What kind of a job?"

"You know . . . a job."

"*That* kind of a job?"

He nodded. She pushed her beer away and went up to the bar, coming back with a cup of coffee in one hand and the pot in the other. "I'll be so sober you won't believe it."

He patted her ass. God, she had a nice ass. "Good girl." They sipped coffee quietly and watched the action around them, anticipation growing in both of them.

You prick, he thought. I'll get you. And the old whore. Tonight. His hand slid around to the front of Priscilla's jeans probing into the warmth, while she grinned, trying to ignore him, sipping her coffee and trying desperately to sober up.

CHAPTER 24

It was dark before Fern had strength enough to get up and get back to the house. She was cold, and walked hunched over, as if each hour on the barn floor had added ten years to her life. She quietly closed the barn door behind her and made her way achingly across the drive and up the porch steps. She must remember to tell Martha about the lifeline to the barn in the winter. That was silly. Martha wouldn't go near the barn. She was afraid. Why was she so afraid?

Martha heard her mother on the porch steps and came out to help her. Her mother looked so old, so frail. In spite of her bulk, she looked sunken and loose. The bun in the back of the old woman's head had come undone, and strands of gray hair trailed behind her.

They shuffled to the bedroom together, and Fern stepped out of her dress and got into bed.

"Whiskey," she whispered to Martha.

Martha brought the bottle and her favorite little glass with mushrooms and birds and flowers on it, poured some, watching Fern's eyes for instructions, and gave it to her. Fern drank it right down, then lay back on the pillows with an exhausted sigh. Soon she was sleeping, and Martha played on the round braided rug at bedside until late. Then she went to bed.

Martha and Fern both woke up with the crow of the cock outside their bedroom windows. Martha padded quietly into her mother's room. Fern held out her trembling hands and quietly asked Martha to get into bed with her. She moved close to her daughter, every movement a chore. She ached all over. Martha was still nice and cuddly-warm from sleep. Fern was so cold.

This is it, she thought. God has given me one more chance. One more try. Please, God, if you've thought anything of my work down here, if I've helped you in any way by easing some of the suffering, grant this old lady one last wish. I'll go in peace, God, if you'll just let me unlock Martha's mind and let her be normal. Please. Don't let her wander around the rest of her life like this, deformed and retarded.

Fern put her left hand on the top of Martha's head. It was cold. It was always the coldest spot on Martha, where it was the warmest on everyone else. Something was blocking that channel of energy. Fern could blast through it if she had the strength, but that might do further damage. Better to loosen it with gentle prodding.

It was an awkward feeling, using her left hand, but she just couldn't manage the shift in position. The life-force energy generally ran through her from left to right. She received information from her left, transmitted it to her right. The healing power came in through her left and out through her right. With her left hand on Martha's head, she was likely to get a good picture of whatever it was Martha had, rather than passing something on to it.

Martha began to fidget. Fern smoothed her hair, talked to her in a low, hoarse voice, trying to settle her down. They'd done this lots of times, with little cuts and scratches, colds, stuffy noses, fevers, and other ailments. Eventually, Martha quieted, lying still and tense, as if she knew something tremendous was about to happen.

Fern was also tense. Afraid. She had never forgotten her last try at this, but now she was old, worn out, dying, and this was her last chance. God could have snuffed her out with a flick of his fingernail last night in the barn, but instead, he had given her one more opportunity to heal. Her most important session was now at hand.

She took a deep breath and began. Her consciousness slipped inside.

She was sinking, falling, spinning around wildly, out of control, diving down, down, down. Fern told herself there was nothing to be afraid of—slow down, my heart. The descent was so swift it brought her stomach to her throat; the blackness was absolute, just the swirling, turning, dizzying fall down a tunnel, a well, a bottomless pit.

Then it opened up, and though she still felt she was falling, now she was falling through a huge black cavern, monstrous in size; she could wave her arms about, her breath wasn't echoed right back to her.

Her descent slowed, much to her wonderment, and she landed lightly on her feet on a roughhewn floor. She paused, slowing her heart, catching her breath, taking a look around. There was nothing to see. Was this the inside of her daughter's mind? It seemed to be more a dream, a fantasy, a movie.

She raised her hands above her head and prayed. A light began to glow. She discovered herself in a tunnel, that same tunnel as before. She walked toward the glow, everything so familiar, so horribly familiar.

She passed the doors, heavy, like oak, and solid. She tried each one as she passed; they didn't budge. Eventually she came to one that hadn't been sealed shut. It was ajar, and Fern pushed gently, and the huge door swung wide open. Fern took a step within and was immediately overcome. It seemed that all the birds in the world were singing cheerful songs. Stained-glass windows shed crystal beauty everywhere she looked. Joy and pleasure coursed through her body in wave after wave. Snatches of melody, little children's songs flashed through her memory; she remembered all of the beauty of life, the happiness, the free, delightful laughter she had once known.

There was something for every sense. The scent of fresh baked bread was there, the smell of rain, bubble bath, perfume, roses. Smiling, open-mouthed, she turned around and around. Every time she shifted her eyes, something new and beautiful appeared before her. Flowers, baby kittens, a fuzzy, tattered red sweater, fresh crayons, and . . . a picture. A picture of Fern, a long time ago, her face fresh and clear, no wrinkles, dark, glossy hair. The face hung there, suspended, completely at home with these other delights, in this room of pleasure. Fern's face. She smiled lovingly at her own face and remembered her mission. She remembered when this door opened, when Martha saw the bubbles in the bath for the first time. She pushed the door wide open to let the merriment course through the hallways of Martha's mind, and left.

The overpowering reality of this room of pleasure stayed with Fern as she continued down the corridor. She tried even harder to open the other doors, pulling, tugging, grunting with the effort. Surely trapped behind each one was Martha's true experience of something— pain maybe, fear, love, understanding, normalcy. Where is the key? Why won't they open?

Gradually she noticed the vibration, the low rumbling. Had it been here all along, or had it just started? She knew the sound, the growl. I must deny the monster, she thought. I must get through to the door of the light. The key must be there. This is my mission. I must unlock these doors! She pushed the fear behind her: I have nothing to fear, I am used up and dead anyway, I must be fearless, *yea, though I walk through the valley of the shadow of death* . . . She began to run. The rumbling grew louder; she heard it take breaths, growling more loudly, more fiercely, threatening. I must get around it.

She saw the door. Translucent, with a soft yellow light emanating from it, lighting up the corridor. The door was closed, and in front of it, standing guard in a protective, attack stance, was the monster.

I must not let it bother me, she thought, intent on her mission. I will not let it distract me. If I look upon it with love in my heart, it cannot hurt me.

Their eyes met, Fern continuing, more slowly now, but steadily. *Thou preparest a table before me in the presence of mine enemies* . . . No quick movements, just fill myself with love, and surround it with peace and easiness, happiness and joy. I'm not here to hurt you; I am here to set my daughter free. The beast snarled, grinned, it seemed, and Fern stopped dead in her tracks. It looks so familiar. Where have I seen that before? She shook her head, rubbing her eyes. Where have I seen that before?

Suddenly she was afraid. As she fought for control, fought to overpower the fear with love, with the knowledge of God's protection, the beast lunged. It struck directly at her chest, sharp teeth biting deep into her heart.

Time slowed. She felt the sharp teeth rip the flesh from her breast, felt the raw stones breaking bones in her back as she fell, the great weight atop her. She saw her outstretched hand claw for the door—short, inches, just inches short—she was not there yet, it was too far away, the beast was chewing on her, God, it was eating her alive, the pain, oh, Martha, the pain, its teeth ripping out her heart, oh, God, so close, so close, oh, God. She looked down, right into the eyes of her attacker, the pain so complete, not the physical pain but the desperation of failure clouding her vision, now it was a man, now it was a dog, now a giant rat, what was it, where oh where did you come from to live within my daughter and at last she knew where she'd seen the beast before.

It was Harry.

CHAPTER 25

"Leon, what's a five-letter word for *solo*? There's an l in it." Martha looked up from her crossword.

"Alone." Leon stood up and clicked off the television. "Like me. I'm going to bed."

"Good idea." Martha wrote the other letters carefully in the squares with her pencil, then closed the book and took off her glasses. He passed behind her, stopping to put his hands on her shoulders as she rubbed her eyes, then he kissed the top of her head.

"C'mon."

"You go ahead. I'll just clean up a bit and be right in."

"Okay."

She heard him brushing his teeth in the bathroom, then the toilet flushed, then the bedsprings creaked as he got in. She picked up crushed beer cans from the new coffee table and wiped it with a towel. What will this house be like without him? She sat for a moment on the new sofa. It was comfortable, and very pretty, in muted colors of browns and golds. There was a new chair to match, and a new rocker, and new draperies. The house looked nice. And it felt nice, with Leon to share it.

She turned off the light and went to bed.

Outside, two pair of eyes watched the light go out. They continued to wait, quietly. Then Priscilla whispered.

"Leslie, what do you think they have that we'd want?"

"Won't know till we get inside."

"Money, you think?"

"That's the only thing worth taking." He paused. "Unless you want to take pictures. Bring a camera?"

Priscilla giggled. He hushed her, then got to his feet. "C'mon."

Sleep was sliding in and around, making a comfortable, cottony womb, as Martha and Leon lay together in the bed. They were soft together, silent, their thoughts running loose, getting ready to give up and sink safely into that timeless place where the cumbersome fetters of awareness were not needed. They were at peace, at rest.

The crash of glass splintered that rest, split it into sharp shards of fear. They sat up as one, Leon reaching for his pants, Martha pulling the covers up to her chin. He flicked on the harsh light and went into the kitchen, and she heard the words, *those* words . . .

"What the fuck are you doing in here?"

Suddenly, she was very small as she moved sideways from the bed, her eyes big and bright, frightened but bold. She moved in her nightgown—it was late, her mommy should have been home by now—bare feet stepping on the cold ground as she made her way into the silent barn.

"Go bring Martha in here, Priscilla," Leslie said as he leveled the gun at Leon. Priscilla's eyes were huge with fright as she did what he told her. He never said he was going to bring a gun.

She slipped past Leon and into the bedroom, where Martha was sliding along the bedroom wall, her eyes wide open but not seeing. "Martha?"

"It's me, Daddy. Mommy's not home yet and I'm afraid."

Oh, Jesus. What is going on in this house?

"I thought I told you never to come into this barn, you little freak." He took a step toward her, into the light, kicking an empty whiskey bottle that went rolling across the floor. He kept coming. He didn't have any clothes on. A little thing dangled between his legs and he was covered in blood. He stopped and turned on the hose, washing himself down, the blood running across the floor toward her feet, running down his legs. He rubbed himself to get it off, and it kept coming toward her toes, her bare toes on the barn floor, and she backed up, and backed up. "Well, you're here now, you want to see what goes on in here? Come here." He pulled on a pair of overalls, then came and grabbed her wrist. "Come here!"

Priscilla grabbed her wrist. "Come here!"

Martha screamed "No! No! I don't want to! Don't make me!" She watched the blood wash toward her, picking up little pieces of hay and bringing it to her, to her toes.

A shot blasted in the living room, more crashing of glass. They were fighting and Priscilla didn't know what to do. She didn't want to go into the living room. And she didn't know what to do with Martha. A heavy thud from the living room. The sounds of fighting stopped, there was heavy breathing, then Leslie's face appeared at the door. He was bleeding from a cut over his eye and had a bruise swelling on one corner of his mouth.

"I told you to come in here!"

"No, Daddy!" Martha whimpered. "I don't want to see."

"You're so all-fired curious about the barn, I *want* you to see." He pulled her across the floor, dragging her feet in the blood; she fell and it got all over her favorite white-lace nightie. He pulled her to the corner where a shallow grave was dug in the dirt, beyond where the cows ate, and there was a baby calf, covered with blood, all crumpled up in the hole. Rats were already dodging in and out taking rips of flesh. She covered her eyes.

"Look at this monster, Martha." He pulled her hands away from her eyes. "Look, damn you! It was born wrong. It was born with two heads. It was a *horror*, Martha, like you. A monster, like you! I had to kill it when it was born, like I should have killed you." He grabbed her nose with hard, calloused fingers that pinched. "Look at this *nose*!"

"Look at this nose," Leslie said, and he pinched it.

His hand hurt her wrist, she twisted to get away, she didn't want to see the thing in the hole, she didn't want the blood, she didn't want any of it. He was hurting her wrist. Her knees collapsed and she sat down hard on the ground, her hand landed on something long and smooth, something that fit her tiny hand, and his face came close to hers, bright eyes and yellow teeth—"Horror! Horror!"—with a terrible stench, a smell of death, of blood, of whiskey, of awful, horrible, and she picked up the hammer and swung it at his head.

Leslie dodged the stool, but it caught Priscilla on the side of the head. Her eyes rolled back and she made a gurgling sound as she landed, twitched for a moment, and then was still.

"Jesus Christ! You killed her!" He stood there for a moment, flexing his hands nervously, then bounced up and down on his toes and ran out of the house.

"You little bitch. Like to kill me, eh? I'll show you what for." He picked her up and threw her in the grave on top of the mutilated body of the calf, rats squeaking and running, then coming back for a smell of the new meat. "Bury the two horrors together," he said, pelting her with clods of dirt. "Bury the two horrors." Then he stopped. He listened for a moment to her frantic whimpering, as she batted at the rats to keep them away from her face, her hands sinking in the still warm ooze of the broken little calf body. Harry put his face in his hands with a moan and ran out.

Martha scrambled out of the grave away from the rodents and that awful thing and whipped off her nightgown, throwing it back in the hole. There was sticky blood all over her, in her hair, on her hands, on her legs; it smelled sweet, tasted salty. She screamed breathlessly, the horses and cows making even more noise, as she ran to the hose and washed herself, frantically, dancing in the cleansing rain—it wouldn't wash away fast enough—and when she was clean, she stood naked and cold in the barn, sobbing, then lay down quietly shivering in the mound of fresh, new hay.

Martha was shivering. She opened her eyes. She was lying naked on top of the bed, still damp from her shower. All the lights were on. She got up slowly to get a fresh nightie from the dresser and almost stepped on Priscilla's lifeless form on the floor.

"Pris! Why you here?" She stooped to help the girl up, but Priscilla's face was a strange blue-gray, and she was cold. A little trickle of blood leaked out one ear and from the side of a small cut at her temple. Martha ran for a washcloth. "S'just blood, Pris. Normal. Happens every time. Here. Clean you up." She sat down with Priscilla's head in her lap and scrubbed at the dried trails until they came clean.

Morning sunlight was coming through the shattered windows when Leon opened his eyes. His head boomed with the light, with his pulse. Shaky fingers sought out the lump like a golf ball on his forehead. Slowly his vision cleared and he remembered Leslie and Priscilla the night before. He raised his pounding head and looked around. The gun was under the coffee table; glass was everywhere. Where was Martha?

Slowly, carefully, he got to his feet, dizzy, every muscle aching, his head feeling like it would either explode or roll right off his shoulders. He stumbled to the bedroom.

He leaned at the doorjamb. Martha was sitting at the dressing table, her back to him. Priscilla's legs stuck out from under the end of the bed.

"Martha?"

She seemed to be humming, putting on makeup. He walked around the edge of the bed.

"Martha?" God, was she all right? "Martha?"

Martha turned to face him, her slack mouth reddened with lipstick and fashioned into a warped smile.

"Leon!"

He took one look and ran for the bathroom, falling to his knees and throwing up everything, his life, his love, his faith, in great heaving gobs of bile. When there was nothing left to come up, he looked toward the door and saw her feet standing in the doorway. He couldn't look at the face. He couldn't look at the face, but in spite of himself, his disbelieving eyes betrayed him and they went directly to her face, to her nose, that huge atrocity that dominated her face, and that thing that hung on it.

He stared, revulsion sweeping him again.

"Leon? Whose sofa?" she asked as she turned to look into the living room.

He retched again, sobbing, crying, not understanding, feeling he'd been cheated in life, cheated out of everything worthwhile, he'd never be the same, never look at things through fresh eyes, he'd been changed, he'd been tainted, he'd been . . .

She kneeled next to him and handed him a tissue to wipe his mouth.

Was it really? He couldn't look. It couldn't be, but his damned eyes again moved directly to her face, and there it was.

Priscilla's nose, once cute and pert, with freckles dancing across it, was now a meaningless, scraped square of gray flesh, tacked somehow to Martha's own impossible nose. Lines of heavy caked makeup surrounded it, even stuck it down in places, but it was beginning to curl and warp from her body heat.

"Oh, Martha," he wailed.

She looked at him, trying to understand, cocking her head back and forth as he stared in disbelief. Then she looked at the sunlight on the floor and guilt crossed her face.

"Oh no," she said, standing up. "Never fed the chickens."

Bigfoot! Killer Cockroaches! Sinister Nuns!
Creepy Kids! Ancient Monsters!

COLLECT THEM ALL!